D0489468

THE

RULES

PAUL ORTON

"You have to learn the rules of the game. And then you have to play better than anyone else."

Albert Einstein

PROLOGUE

Rain lashed down as the boy ran along the road in total darkness, struggling to see the way ahead. The trees on either side gave no shelter from the downpour.

He looked exhausted, but also desperate. His clothes were soaked, his face streaked with mud. In one hand he clutched a small device wrapped in plastic.

There was a burning sensation in his lungs. His body screamed at him to stop, to take a break. He ignored it. He had to make it to the gates.

Just keep running, he told himself, forcing one foot in front of another. *Don't stop!*

'I'm nearly there,' he shouted over the wind and rain. 'I have what you want! Don't kill him!'

There was no response; he was alone.

This was his last chance. He couldn't afford to make another mistake. Not when lives hung in the balance.

He'd never be able to forgive himself.

So he kept on running through the driving rain and on into the night.

1. MISTAKE

Ryan snapped the pencil and began tearing at the splintered wood with his teeth. In theory at least, everything was going well, but the computer was taking way too long.

The house was quiet and empty. Marcus liked his music on full blast when he was working, but Ryan could only focus when it was silent. And right now, he needed to focus.

'Come on, come on,' he muttered, leaning closer to the screen and frowning. After several lines of complicated code, a dialogue box showed the words 'Application SpidersWeb 68% complete...'

It was *so slow*.

Ryan stood up, kicking his school bag across the room in frustration. 9.12pm and it wasn't ready. If it took much longer, he'd have to call it off.

'Application SpidersWeb 72% complete...'

He tore his attention away from the program, caving in to the distressed groaning coming from his stomach.

Stepping over his abandoned school uniform and dirty football kit, he made his way on to the landing.

His parents were at some charity dinner and he was home alone. That suited him fine; hours of uninterrupted time with no pressure to sit down for a family meal or hassle about chores. But with those bonuses came the lack of home-cooked food.

He padded his way down to the kitchen. The house was kind of creepy when it was empty, despite the ultra-modern decor. He turned on the bright kitchen spotlights, illuminating gleaming white units and black granite worktop. It was immaculate, as always. Ryan's room was the exception; the cleaner wouldn't touch that. The state of it drove his parents mad, but as he always argued, it was *his* room.

Ryan slid along the floor and looked inside the fridge. The microwave meal his parents had left him sat on the top shelf untouched. Ignoring it, he grabbed a can and a chocolate bar and raced back upstairs.

The message on the screen had changed: 'Application SpidersWeb 100% complete. Run (Y/N)?'

Ryan hit the 'Y' key. A new line appeared: 'Spider's Web active. Input target.'

Finally.

He copied out several numbers, separated by full stops. The screen behind the command prompt window changed to give a clear warning: "THIS IS A SECURE SITE. AUTHORISED ACCESS ONLY. Attempting to log in to this system is a criminal act. Offenders will be arrested and prosecuted under the Terrorism Act."

Ryan grinned. 'Yeah, right.'

He typed the critical command: 'Run Mites.exe'.

And then he waited. At first he thought the program had crashed, but after a few tense seconds, the screen changed. At the top were the words: 'Ministry of Defence Secure System'.

He let out a wild whoop in celebration and disbelief. He'd done it. Now he needed proof. Taking a quick swig of his drink, he got to work.

It took him twenty minutes to find an impressive-looking file and start downloading it. Outside, in the real world, he heard the slam of a car door. Then another. His parents were back.

Or were they?

Ryan had a nagging sense that something wasn't right. He wanted to ignore it and stay focused on the hack, but felt too tense. He had to check it out.

Tearing himself away from the screen, he sidled onto the landing and peeked through a small gap in the curtains, looking out at the front garden and dimly lit street.

Danger. A black van had pulled up. Five dark figures were moving along the driveway in the darkness.

His heart thudded in his chest. He ran back to the computer and held down a few keys, so it started deleting the evidence. A deafening smash echoed through the house as the front door caved in, filling the hallway with broken glass and splintered wood. These guys meant business!

Ryan scrambled on to the desk and pushed open the large window behind. Clinging to the window frame, he slid his body out and tried lowering himself down. The ground looked a long way off, but it was his only chance of escape.

Taking a deep breath, he let go.

Impact. He landed on a flower-bed, rolling sideways in the mud. His mum would go mad when she saw what he'd done to her precious lavender, but that was the last of his worries. He was up and running, his heart pounding, adrenaline fuelling his movements. For a few glorious seconds, he thought he had a chance.

But he was wrong.

Half-way across the lawn, he was rugby-tackled to the ground and his face pressed hard in the dirt. His hands were held firmly behind his back and cold metal cuffs clicked shut around his wrists. Then he was hauled back on his feet as if he was made of polystyrene.

The man who'd captured him looked like a soldier, but was wearing all-black combats rather than standard camouflage. He said nothing, but checked Ryan's jeans, pulling out his brand-new phone.

'Hey, give that back!'

The man locked eyes with him and slipped it into his pocket.

Ryan felt like his soul had been ripped out. 'What the hell? You can't take that! Who are you?'

'Quiet.' The soldier pushed him towards the gate. Ryan tried to pull away, but the man's hand was like a vice.

As they rounded the corner, Ryan saw other soldiers moving in and out of the house. None of them spoke. His computer was being carried out: all of it, monitor included. Then his dad's laptop. They took cables, accessories, everything. Hopefully, all the evidence had been deleted from the hard drive before they got to it. Otherwise, he was screwed.

A sudden gust of wind made Ryan shiver, his faded sleeveless t-shirt offering him little protection. His stylish jeans always hung low at the back, both to show off his designer underwear and to irritate his parents, but right now they were too low, even by his standards. He tugged them up as he stumbled along, but with his hands cuffed behind him, he only made them more uncomfortable.

The adrenaline high was wearing off, and he realised he didn't have any shoes on. His thin socks were wet, and his feet were freezing.

'I need my trainers!' he said, but the soldier ignored him. He was dragged towards the van and pushed inside. Ryan fell forwards, banging his knees, before being hauled on to a seat and strapped in. 'Watch out! I'm just a kid!'

It didn't seem to matter. Within seconds, two other soldiers joined them. They sat on either side of Ryan. The door slid shut, and the vehicle started to move.

Ryan squirmed and glanced up at the expressionless faces. 'Is this meant to scare me?' he asked, trying to sound tough.

One soldier looked at him but didn't respond.

'At least let me out of these cuffs!' insisted Ryan, fidgeting.

'No chance,' said the soldier. 'If I were you, I'd get

used to those.'

Ryan swore under his breath.

This was not good.

2. TROUBLE

Ryan shivered in the gloom. For some sinister reason, the chair he sat on was bolted to the floor. Dark-grey breeze-block walls seemed to suck away the light coming from the dim bulb that hung overhead. The room was empty. There were no windows, and the reinforced steel door was studded with giant rivets. You could keep a gorilla in here. He had expected some sort of interview room, but this was like a cell. It wasn't a good sign.

The journey had taken over an hour. The vehicles had stopped at a security gate staffed by soldiers. There was a chain-link fence with coils of barbed wire. He was half-walked, half-dragged into a featureless concrete building, down a blank corridor and then left here.

Ryan had been afraid at first—terrified, in fact. He imagined a hundred different ways they might torture him. Then he'd forced himself to calm down. They might be hardcore, but there were limits. He was a minor. They were trying to scare him, and they were doing a good job, but it was just mind games.

He figured that at least an hour had passed, and he was getting tired as well as hungry. He looked up at the camera in the corner. 'You can't do this! I'm only thirteen!' he shouted, unsure if anyone could hear him. 'My dad will sue you, do you hear me? You'll get arrested for child abuse!'

There was no response. They'd have to find out the hard way. How long were they going to leave him? He was probably going to miss the match tomorrow. Pascal and the others would be angry with him, but what could he do? They'd never believe any of this.

Only Marcus would know that he wasn't lying: he knew what Ryan was capable of. But even Marcus would be impressed that he'd hacked the Ministry of Defence. He'd also laugh at him for being so stupid. The first lesson of hacking, he said, was not getting caught. He'd tease Ryan about it when he found out, his know-it-all tone grating on Ryan's ego.

Ryan shivered again, wishing he at least had his hoodie. His stomach made a groaning sound, protesting at the lack of any decent meal since lunchtime. He was losing all feeling in his hands.

'Come on!' he shouted. 'Are you gonna charge me or what?'

To his surprise, he heard the clicking of the lock. An older woman walked in, wearing a smart military uniform which gave Ryan the impression that she was important. A soldier followed her, holding a large gun.

More mind games.

Ryan wasn't in the mood to play.

The officer towered over him, a file in her hands. Ryan stared back, trying not to show any guilt or fear.

If he was lucky, she might think he was a stupid kid. He knew he looked young for his age. Maybe he could use that to his advantage.

'Ryan Jacobs,' she stated. 'Thirteen years old. You attend Highview Comprehensive School. You live in the suburbs. You're from a well-off family.' She flicked through the file before continuing. 'We've been watching you for some time. You probed our system a couple of months back, but never launched a proper attack. Tonight, that changed. You broke through our defences.'

'I don't know what you're talking about,' Ryan insisted. 'I was playing computer games and then these guys came into the house...'

'Don't be difficult, Ryan. We know everything. The evidence is all over your hard drive. You hacked our system. That means you present a threat to our national security.'

Ryan sighed, leaned forward, and looked down at the floor. Game over. It seemed there was no point denying it. 'You should let me go,' he muttered. 'Or my dad will sue you. You're in enough trouble as it is.'

The woman laughed, making Ryan's cheeks burn. 'It's you who's in trouble, Ryan. Your dad can't get you out of this. I suggest you start co-operating.'

He was out of his depth, but he wasn't one to give up. He stayed silent.

'Hungry?' asked the woman after a brief pause.

Ryan glanced up at her. 'A bit,' he admitted.

'I can get you some food. And drink. But first you need to tell me what you've been up to.'

'Why?' shot back Ryan. 'Apparently you already know everything.'

The woman scowled, and Ryan shifted in his seat.

'Let me make this perfectly clear,' she said. 'I ask the questions here, and you answer them. We know *what* you did, not *how* you did it. Now start talking.'

'Screw you.' Ryan sounded a lot more confident than he felt.

'You'll tell us in the end. You may as well save yourself a lot of suffering.'

'Yeah, what you gonna do? I have rights. I know you can't hurt me.'

The woman took a step back, closed the file and stashed it under her arm. 'Have it your way.' She started towards the door.

'Wait, where are you going?' Ryan could hear the desperation in his own voice. He sounded weak and cowardly.

'I'm going to bed, Ryan. Perhaps you'll be more co-operative in the morning. I'll see you in, say, eight hours?' She opened the door and made to step out.

'But what about food?' Ryan called after her. 'And getting out of these handcuffs? And a bed? You can't leave me like this!'

The woman paused. 'We can't hurt you, Ryan. You're right. But under the Terrorism Act we can hold you here for as long as we want. And things here can happen *really slowly*.' She emphasised the last two words in a way that made Ryan shudder. 'I'm sure that we'll take the handcuffs off eventually, and you'll get something for breakfast, but I'm not going to lie to you: the food here isn't great. It's often dry or burnt. Yours might be especially bad, if you catch my meaning?'

Ryan grimaced before he could stop himself.

'You'll get moved to a holding cell as soon as the paperwork is processed,' she continued, 'but it's a complicated form, so what can I do? It could take all night. And even then, the cell you'll be moved to won't have the luxury bedding you're used to. We don't have special cells for children and sometimes the people we lock up have *accidents*.'

Ryan gave the woman a scathing look, wondering if she was bluffing. 'You can't do that. I don't believe you.'

'I don't care.' The woman turned back towards the door.

Ryan realised he couldn't take the risk. 'Fine,' he called out, furious with himself. 'I'll talk.'

It wasn't fine. He'd broken way too easily. But the thought of staying in that room with an empty stomach and his hands chained behind his back was too much to take.

The woman walked back towards him, standing too close for Ryan's comfort. 'How did you do it, Ryan?'

Ryan looked at her, at the wrinkles on her face and her greying hair. She was a dinosaur. There was no way she'd understand the finer points of system security.

'It was a SPE override attack, using a purpose-built algorithm.' Ryan raised his eyebrows. 'Do you want me to spell that out for you? I mean, have you ever used a computer?'

'Once or twice.' The woman's lip curled. She was amused, not annoyed. 'We're going to need a bit more detail, but I think you've at least earned your way out of those cuffs.'

She made a signal to the soldier, who stepped behind Ryan and unlocked them. Ryan rubbed his numb wrists.

'Now, before we get into the nuts and bolts of your hack,' she continued, 'do you want to tell me *why* you'd want to do it in the first place?'

Ryan shrugged and looked away. 'Just because. It's fun, I guess.'

'It's fun.' The woman repeated it as though Ryan was the stupidest kid she'd ever met. She'd make an excellent teacher, thought Ryan, the sort that humiliates kids when they mess around.

'Are you part of any kind of group?'

'No. I work alone.'

She was about to ask another question when the door was thrown open and a silver-haired guy walked in. A crewcut and a couple of old scars on his cheek made him appear tough, like he'd been in a lot of fights. He was tall, too—much taller than either the soldier or the other officer. He clearly outranked them both, and they saluted.

'At ease, Major Atherton,' growled the newcomer. 'I'm here to take the kid.'

'Of course, Colonel, but... we haven't worked out how he did it yet.'

'*Our* guys have.' The colonel left no room for disagreement. He handed the major a form. 'Here's the transfer order.'

Major Atherton checked it through but seemed to have no grounds for objection. 'Ok, Colonel, he's all yours.'

'Thank you.' The colonel looked at Ryan as if he'd scraped him off his shoe. 'For what it's worth, I don't particularly *want* him, but orders are orders.' He grabbed Ryan by his upper arm and yanked him to his feet.

'Hey, careful!' said Ryan. 'I'm not resisting here.'

The colonel didn't reply. He dragged him out of the room and down a long corridor. Ryan had to jog to keep up.

They headed outside. A military helicopter sat a short distance from the building, its rotors spinning. The noise was deafening.

'I hope you're afraid of heights, boy!' shouted the colonel as he pushed Ryan towards it.

'No.' Ryan wouldn't have admitted it, even if he was.

'Pity.' The man threw Ryan into the back and sat opposite. He slid the door shut and looked away in disgust.

There was one other person in the back who helped Ryan with the seatbelt as they lifted off. This guy looked out of place in the military surroundings, wearing a bright flowery shirt and cream trousers. He was pretty old, small and thin—not that much bigger than Ryan himself.

'I'm Mr Davids,' he said, smiling.

'I'm Ryan. Ryan Jacobs.'

'Yes, yes, I know.' The man pointed at the laptop on the other side of him. 'I've just been examining your work.'

3. ARRIVAL

The journey was long and uncomfortable.

Ryan had expected the helicopter to be posh inside, but it was like his school minibus. The seats were torn, the fake-leather coverings tatty. In the limited light, he could see dirt all over the floor. It smelt of stale sweat, oil and mud—a combination that made his stomach queasy.

He wondered where they going. Fortunately, Mr Davids did a great job of distracting him, babbling away about the hack like a small child showing off his favourite toy.

'So you've produced an algorithm that attacks from different points on the grid simultaneously... it's quite incredible. At thirteen as well? And no-one taught you how to do this? Spider mites indeed. What an imagination!'

Ryan felt patronised, but Mr Davids had gained access to the mites code, which meant he'd somehow back-hacked the program. Ryan had been out-classed by this guy and that demanded a grudging respect, despite the flowery shirt.

With the briefest of pauses, the man was off again. 'The mites are pretty elegant little programs. I'm guessing you hoped that a multiple hack from so many locations at once would prevent them from tracing you?'

'That was the plan,' Ryan said bitterly. 'It appears it didn't work.'

'It nearly did.' Mr Davids paused and pushed his glasses back up his nose. 'Few systems could resist that kind of attack. I once designed a program not that dissimilar to this one myself. It's exceptional. Quite exceptional.'

Ryan figured he might as well try to learn something. 'How did you trace me?' he asked.

'Ah, well, it's interesting you should ask. You see...'

'That's confidential,' interrupted the colonel. 'Don't you dare tell him.'

'No, no, of course. You're right.' Mr Davids clammed up. Ryan was disappointed. The old computer guy caught his eye and winked, but he said nothing further, and they travelled the rest of the way in silence.

Ryan looked out the window but could only see tiny lights far below. Reflected in the glass, he caught a glimpse of the colonel glaring at him. If he had his way, Ryan would fall out of the helicopter in a freak accident.

Eventually, they began to descend. A hard bump reverberated through the cockpit as they touched down. Seconds later, the colonel slid open the door, then leaned over and pressed the release on Ryan's belt.

'Out,' he said, as if saving his words for people

who mattered.

Ryan jumped down. He misjudged the distance in the darkness and ended up sprawled on all fours. As he got up, he saw he was in the grounds of a large mansion. It looked like the kind of place you'd pay to visit.

The colonel grabbed hold of him and forced him forward, up a gravel driveway, the sharp stones digging into his feet. He didn't say anything, refusing to let the colonel see any weakness.

They climbed the smooth stone steps. The front door opened into a vast hallway with an impressive staircase. Everything looked antique and expensive. Ryan's mum would have loved it. The thought of her sent a brief panic coursing through him. What would she be thinking right now? Had anyone told his parents where he was?

A woman walked towards them in a white lab coat, her heels making a crisp clicking noise on the hard floor. 'Good evening, Colonel,' she said. 'A successful trip, I see?'

'I'm not sure I'd call it successful, Doctor,' the colonel grumbled. 'I will make an official complaint to the Board. There are better places for scum like him.'

'You will be able to state your case, of course,' she replied, 'but right now, let's follow protocol. What's his name?'

'I'm Ryan.'

'Jacobs,' interrupted the colonel. 'His name is Jacobs.'

'Jacobs, my name is Dr Fleur. Come with me.' She

didn't seem friendly, but as far as Ryan was concerned, anything was better than being dragged around by the colonel.

She took him down a long corridor and into a plain white tiled room, which looked like a doctor's surgery. There was an examination table, a running machine and a small desk with a computer. Ryan eyed it with interest.

'Sit down, Jacobs. I'm going to check your pulse and blood pressure.'

'Where am I?' he asked, perching on the edge of a blue plastic chair.

'Everything will be explained in the morning.' She strapped the monitor to his arm, and it started to inflate.

'What about my parents? They'll be worried. Don't I get a phone call?'

'We have informed your parents of where you are. You will speak to them tomorrow.' That was good news, if it was true.

Dr Fleur finished taking the reading and unstrapped the monitor. 'A little high,' she observed, 'but that's hardly surprising in the circumstances.'

No kidding, thought Ryan.

'Can I at least have something to eat?' he asked. 'I'm starving.'

'First, I need to test your fitness. Step over here.' She gestured to the running machine in the corner.

Ryan shuffled over. 'Can't we do this in the morning? I'm kind of tired.'

'That's not relevant.'

'Yeah, well it's relevant to me!' He was sick of no-one listening to him. Dr Fleur raised her eyebrows. Ryan got the impression she wasn't used to being spoken to like that.

'If you want food, Jacobs, then you can earn it. Keep running for the next twenty minutes. If you slow the machine down or stop, then you stay hungry.'

'Seriously?' said Ryan. What kind of doctor was she? He scrambled round for an excuse. 'I can't run in jeans.'

'Then take them off. No-one's going to see you.'

Ryan hesitated. It seemed that Dr Fleur wasn't going to negotiate. 'Fine.' He slipped off his jeans and stepped on.

Dr Fleur pressed a button, and the treadmill began to move. She set him off at a brisk walk. Once he'd warmed up, she increased the speed.

'Hey, that's too fast,' he gasped.

'I decide that,' she replied. She pressed the button a few more times. By now, Ryan was breaking a sweat. The doctor watched him for a few minutes before she spoke again. 'I need to pop out to get your food. Remember, no slowing down and no stopping. Let's see how long you can sustain that kind of exertion.'

As soon as she'd left, Ryan glanced around. He couldn't see any cameras. No way was he going to keep running like a stupid hamster. This might be his last chance at freedom before they locked him up. It was time he got answers.

He jumped off the treadmill and stumbled over to

25

the door. As he'd expected, it was locked, operated by a fingerprint scanner, but they'd need more than that to keep him prisoner. He sat down at the computer in the corner, moving the mouse to bring the monitor to life, revealing a secure login screen.

Trying common passwords would be a waste of time: no-one would use anything that easy in a place like this. He'd have to use a backdoor. Holding down two of the keys, he rebooted it. That gave him access to the machine registry where he could alter a few of the values. He lost valuable minutes as it restarted, but it was worth it: this time the computer thought he was an administrator and he could gain access.

Now came the hard part: finding something useful. Hidden in the network would be information which might help him escape. It took a while hunting through, but in a folder labelled 'Security' he located a floor plan of the building. It was titled 'Devonmoor Academy Site Plan'. So, this was a school—probably a place for young offenders.

Thinking about the route he'd followed from the entrance hall, he could identify the room he was in. He accessed the security system and activated a test protocol. The small light by the door-sensor changed from red to green.

After dragging on his jeans, Ryan opened the door and checked the corridor. It was deserted. Was he going to do this? He figured he couldn't get in any worse trouble. He might as well take his chances.

It was only a short distance to the nearest fire exit. As he pushed open the doors an alarm sounded.

Ryan cursed and darted outside into the cool night air.

The grounds were darker than he was expecting. He was almost too afraid to go any further, but he had to press on. If he couldn't see anything then neither could anyone who was trying to find him. Besides, if he kept running, he was bound to come to a fence or wall. It wasn't the best plan he'd ever had, but he was tired and hungry and annoyed so it would have to do.

'Freeze.' Ryan had barely stepped onto the lawn when he heard the warning. He turned to see a soldier standing a fair distance away. The man was pointing a gun at Ryan's chest. 'Don't move.'

Ryan narrowed his eyes, a sceptical look on his face. 'Sure, so if I run, you'll shoot me? Even though I'm a teenager?'

'If I have to,' warned the soldier, stepping closer.

'You know what?' said Ryan. 'I don't believe you!'

He backed away. He figured he could get to the trees before the soldier could catch him. As Ryan moved, the soldier took aim.

'This is your last warning, kid.' The man didn't sound nervous.

'Yeah? Well do it then!' demanded Ryan, taking another step while holding out his arms. 'I dare you! Stop talking and shoot me! Come on!'

'Ok,' shrugged the soldier. 'If you insist.'

Then, he fired.

4. ANSWERS

The siren was way too loud. Ryan half-opened his eyes to see what was making the racket, then jerked awake as he remembered what had happened.

He was lying on the bottom bunk in a small dormitory. Three lads had jumped out of bed and were pulling on identical clothes: a dark grey uniform with a thin maroon stripe down each side. The collar was military. They didn't appear to be young offenders, more like army cadets.

His head hurt. He groaned as he realised that he'd been shot with a tranquilliser dart. They'd knocked him out and brought him here for the night.

'Check it out! A new boy!' One lad pointed at Ryan and the other two turned to look.

'Hi, I'm Lee.' The lad with short, blond hair introduced himself.

'I'm Ryan.' He sat up and pushed back the duvet, stopping half-way as he realised he was naked.

'What happened to you?' asked one of the other lads. 'Did they find you in a ditch?'

'It's a long story.'

'I'm Kev by the way.' He was handsome and solidly built, and he spoke with a posh accent. 'This is Jael.' He pointed at a thin Hispanic lad with glasses who was busy tugging up his trousers.

'Where am I?' Ryan asked. 'Is this a place for young offenders?' They glanced at each other with amusement, making him feel stupid.

'No, mate,' laughed Lee. 'It's a school, of sorts. How can you not know that?'

'Are you serious?' asked Jael, taking a genuine interest for the first time. 'You don't know where you are? How did you get here?'

'Like I said, it's a long story. I'm kind of confused right now.'

'We don't have time for this,' Kev interrupted. 'Come on, we're gonna be late.'

'Do we just leave him here?' asked Lee, concerned. 'He doesn't know where he is.'

'Forget it, Lee.' Kev was already heading out the door. 'Not our problem.'

'Fine.' Lee turned to Ryan, apologetically. 'There are clean clothes in the wardrobe over there. Help yourself. I'll catch up with you later.'

'Thanks.'

Lee shot off after the others.

Now he was alone, Ryan climbed out of bed. The dorm didn't hold any surprises. It had two sets of bunk beds, two cupboards and a chest of drawers. In the corner was a door through to a small bathroom.

He checked himself in the mirror. His face was streaked with mud and his hair was a complete mess. He washed in the sink and borrowed a comb. There was no gel, but he made it look at least half-decent.

Now for some clothes. The cupboards were full of

grey uniforms and old-fashioned rugby kits: nothing that he wanted to wear. Still, he had to put something on.

He pulled on a white vest followed by the military trousers and jacket, just as the other lads had done. There were some ridiculously long grey socks: if he pulled them up he had to fold them down at the knee, so he left them bunched around his ankles. The shiny black boots were also too big for him, but they were better than nothing.

What now? Ryan pulled back the curtains. An area of cultivated lawn gave way to hedges and trees further back. It all looked peaceful in the morning sun. There were no bars, no chain-link fences; it was nothing like the place he'd expected to end up in.

'Jacobs.' The voice startled him and he spun around. Dr Fleur was standing in the doorway. 'Come with me. Unless you're too busy planning your next escape?' She looked amused.

'No, I'm good.'

'Wise decision.' She set off down the corridor and Ryan followed. 'Where are we going?'

'I'm taking you to Lady Devonmoor.'

'Who's that?'

'The head-teacher. She'll be able to answer your questions.'

Ryan hoped so.

***

Lady Devonmoor's office was enormous. A

fireplace dominated one wall and two large windows looked out onto the front lawn. Floral sofas and chairs formed a meeting area in the middle. At one end, sitting at an enormous desk, was an elderly woman, small with white hair. Her face was wrinkled, making her eyes and mouth appear as if they were permanently smiling. She stood up as he entered.

'You must be Ryan,' she said, warmly. 'I'm Lady Devonmoor. It's so good to see you my dear. I imagine you have a lot of questions. Come, sit with me.'

She gestured towards the armchairs in front of the window. Ryan slumped into one.

'I see you're already fitting in well,' she said, indicating the uniform. 'It suits you.'

'I guess,' replied Ryan, caught off guard. This place was full of surprises. He'd expected something military or hostile. He thought he'd have to talk with the colonel or a mysterious man in a black suit.

'Would you like a cup of tea?' she asked, leaning towards a side table where a porcelain teapot waited along with china cups, a milk jug and a sugar bowl.

'No,' said Ryan, 'all I want is answers.'

Lady Devonmoor poured a cup for herself and added a dash of milk. 'You must be wondering where you are?'

'Too right. What is this place?'

'This is Devonmoor Academy,' she announced, a note of pride in her voice. 'It's a school, a rather special school for the most intelligent and able young people in the country. But it's also much more than

31

that. It's an experiment that my grandfather started over seventy years ago. That's him up there.' She pointed to the picture.

Ryan didn't look; he couldn't care less about her family history. 'What do you mean by *experiment*?' he asked.

'He called it the Project. My grandfather knew young people think differently to adults. Some children in particular have gifts and skills that need to be nurtured. If taught carefully, and encouraged to work together, these young people could hold the key to solving the most tricky problems we face as a country, or even as a species.'

Ryan wasn't impressed. It sounded like the plot for a terrible B-Movie. 'That's insane.'

'You're not the first person to say that,' said Lady Devonmoor. 'In fact, he had quite a lot of difficulty convincing others of it. But he was a clever and stubborn man, and he had considerable influence. He stuck to his guns and founded this academy.'

'Good for him.' Ryan acted disinterested.

'No, Ryan, not just good for him. Good for all of us. He knew that when you gather together a highly skilled group of students and give them exceptional teachers and the space to think creatively, you can develop new kinds of solutions to the most complex problems. That's what the Project is all about. Our country and our world need this place.'

'If you say so.'

'I *know* so,' said the old lady. 'He's been proved right again and again. Over the last seventy years, this academy has been the source of some amazing scientific discoveries and technological break-throughs. That's why the government fund and support the Project. They know its true value.'

'Yeah? So how come I've never heard of it?' Ryan was finding it all hard to believe.

'Because it's one of the country's most closely guarded secrets,' explained the head-teacher. 'Imagine the problems if they made it public: an elite school for the brightest kids, a hub of new discoveries. Every parent would think their kid should get a place. Then there are the projects we work on, the technology we use. And the fact that over the years we've picked up a few enemies. The secrecy keeps us safe. From the outside it looks like any other private school. Only a few people know the truth.'

'Well, even if that's all true,' said Ryan, 'what's any of it got to do with me?'

'Ryan, dear, you are very bright. Mr Davids says you show tremendous potential with computers, and he would know. There isn't a system in the world that can keep him out for long!' Ryan could believe that. 'He says that the way in which you carried out your hack shows a level of lateral thinking and creativity which is nothing short of remarkable, and that you will be a valuable asset to Devonmoor.'

Ryan wasn't used to that kind of praise. He found it hard to keep his defences up. 'I didn't ask to come here.'

'No, dear, but once you've seen what we have to offer you'll love it! Here at the academy you'll get teaching and opportunities that you can't get anywhere else.'

And stupid amounts of work, thought Ryan. He didn't need that kind of pressure in his life. 'I'm not staying,' he replied. 'I can't. My parents won't let it happen.'

'You don't need to worry about that.' Lady Devonmoor took a sip of her tea. 'Your parents will arrive shortly and they will be quite happy with the arrangement.'

Ryan doubted that very much.

'What could be more of a problem,' she added, 'is persuading the Board. They can be very selective.'

'The Board?' Ryan couldn't keep up.

'It's the group of people that oversee the Project. They decide who can be a part of it and make all the big decisions.'

'And they don't want me here?'

'They haven't decided yet. But you're a little unusual, even for a Devonmoor student.'

'Yeah? Why's that?'

Lady Devonmoor paused, pondering her next words. 'Let's just say that most of our students don't get into trouble. Discipline is a big deal here. It has to be, given what's at stake. I think you'd need to convince the Board that you could follow the rules.'

'Screw that,' shrugged Ryan. 'I don't need to convince them of anything. I'm going home with my parents.'

'We'll see.' Lady Devonmoor smiled. 'We won't find out until they get here, so why not take time this morning to get to know the place a little. See what you think. I'll call for you when your parents arrive.'

'Sure. I guess.' It wasn't like he had much choice.

The head-teacher stood up and pressed a buzzer. Lee walked into the room, stood to attention and saluted. It was weird to see a kid his age do that.

'Lee, take Ryan to breakfast will you?' said Lady Devonmoor. 'Then let him accompany you to your lessons.'

'Yes, ma'am.'

Ryan followed him out of the room, his head spinning. He didn't know what to make of it all. The only thing he knew for sure was that he was desperate for some food.

Breakfast sounded good.

5. GRUEL

The canteen bustled with students. Roughly a hundred of them, aged from eleven to seventeen, a mixture of boys and girls. Everyone wore the same uniform but, unlike at Ryan's school, they all looked smart. No shirts hung out of trousers and no-one wore trainers instead of shoes.

Most of them sat at long tables. The boys joined the queue to the serving area at the far end. Ryan could smell bacon and eggs and his stomach growled in anticipation.

'Sorry we couldn't talk earlier,' said Lee. 'We had to get to drill. You get punished if you're late.'

'No worries,' Ryan assured him. 'Thanks for the clothes.'

'You'll get your own soon enough.' Lee was matter-of-fact about it.

'No I won't. I'm not staying.'

'Really? Why not? This place is awesome!'

'It looks too strict for my liking.'

'It's alright,' said Lee. 'I mean, there are a lot of rules and they're pretty strict about uniform and stuff, but you soon get used to it.'

'Yeah, well I don't need to,' replied Ryan. 'I'm going home this afternoon.'

'Ok, but you're missing out.'

In the corner, the colonel was standing chatting to an older boy—a tall, mean-looking lad with a shaved head. The conversation ended, and the colonel left. That guy gave him the creeps.

As he looked around, Ryan spotted a few cadets wearing black berets. 'Why do some students get hats?' he asked.

'Prefects,' explained Lee. 'It's a big deal here. They have almost as much power as the teachers. You have to do what they say or you get into serious trouble.'

'Right.' Ryan had no intention of doing what anyone told him, but he didn't feel the need to point that out.

A few minutes later, they reached the front of the queue. Each student spent a short time at a computer console before going forward to collect their food.

'What's with the screens?'

'We do a kind of test,' said Lee. 'If you do well then you get whatever food you want.'

'What if you don't do so well?'

'Don't worry, you'll be fine. If you weren't clever, you wouldn't be here.'

Ryan wasn't sure that was true, but one screen was free and Lee nudged him towards it. There was a single button: 'START TEST'. Ryan pressed it while Lee took his place at the console next to him.

The first question flashed up: 'What is the relationship between Pi and Tau?' Below it were three options: 'A. Pi is 0.5 x Tau. B. Tau is the square root of Pi. C. Tau is 0.5 x Pi.' Ryan didn't know which to choose.

'Hey Lee,' he muttered. 'What's the first one?'

'Quiet,' urged Lee. 'We'll get into trouble.'

He sounded worried. Ryan didn't care about the school or its rules, but he didn't want to create problems for his new friend. Besides, it was multiple choice; he could guess.

He hit the second option. It wasn't correct. A red cross appeared and then another question: 'In the periodic table, which element comes below Germanium?' The possible answers were gold, carbon, lead or tin. Ryan guessed again. Wrong again.

There were three other questions, all in quick succession. He continued choosing at random, only getting one right. A red ticket appeared from a slot to the right of the screen: 'Please take the ticket and proceed.'

Well, at least that was over.

'How did you do?' asked Lee.

Ryan showed him his ticket.

'A red? You got a red? That's bad.'

'I don't care,' shrugged Ryan. 'I just need breakfast.'

One of the canteen staff looked at Lee who held up a yellow slip. 'What would you like, cadet?' she asked.

'Full breakfast please, no mushrooms,' replied Lee. The woman dished up bacon, eggs, sausages and beans on to Lee's plate.

She then turned to Ryan. 'Your ticket?'

Ryan held it up. He watched with horror as she filled a bowl with dry cereal, poured water on it and handed it to him.

'What's this?' he asked. 'Where's the bacon and eggs? I want proper food.'

'You're lucky you've got anything at all,' said the woman. 'Move on.'

'Look, Ryan,' said Lee, pulling on his arm. 'You have to do better in the test if you want good food. It's an incentive, see?'

'This place is insane.' Ryan's stomach tightened as he looked at the contents of his bowl. He'd been looking forward to a cooked breakfast so much, and now he had this slop.

'Let's get a seat,' urged Lee. They walked over to a table. Some of the other cadets had a cooked breakfast; others had toast, fruit or muesli. No-one had anything that looked as bad as his.

'What kind of place tests you before breakfast?' he asked.

'This isn't a normal school. You have to work twice as hard here.' Lee was trying to make it sound ok.

'I don't *need* to do anything Lee. I'll be leaving as soon as my parents arrive.' Ryan took a spoonful of the cereal and crunched it. It tasted of nothing. It was as horrible as it looked. He made a face of disgust.

Lee glanced around to see if anyone was watching before leaning over and taking the bowl, handing him the cooked breakfast in its place. 'Here, have this,' he said. 'It might cheer you up.'

Ryan softened a little at the sacrifice Lee was willing to make. He had done nothing to deserve it. 'I can't eat this. It's yours,' he objected. 'I appreciate it and everything but I wouldn't want anyone to have to eat *that*.'

'It's fine mate,' said Lee. 'You look hungry. Besides, this isn't that bad.'

'If you're sure.' Ryan didn't want to push the point. He was painfully aware that he hadn't eaten the previous night. He took a mouthful of bacon and then a thought struck him. 'What happens if you get *all* the questions wrong?'

'You get *really* hungry,' Lee replied, taking another spoonful of the cereal. 'Like I said, this isn't that bad.'

This was the strangest school Ryan had ever heard of. It was all a bit messed up. Was it even legal? 'So how did you end up here, anyway?' he asked Lee.

'I learn stuff fast and I'm good at remembering things, so they offered me a scholarship.'

'You *wanted* to come here?'

Before Lee had a chance to answer, the conversation was interrupted. Cold liquid ran through Ryan's hair and down his back. He turned to see the tall youth with the shaved head standing behind him, a wicked grin on his face.

'What did you do that for?' Ryan shouted, standing up. All eyes were on him. Everyone stopped talking; they wanted to see how this would play out.

'Apologies, new boy,' said the cadet, his voice dripping with sarcasm. 'I accidentally spilled my drink.

So sorry. It's such a shame to see a uniform get ruined. But then again, as you're a criminal the fact that you're wearing it did rather spoil it, anyway.'

Ryan had dealt with bullies before. He didn't argue. He didn't hesitate. Without warning, he launched himself at the lad, punching him hard in the stomach. To Ryan's surprise, his opponent didn't even flinch.

'Is that the best you've got?' he taunted. 'My little sister can hit harder than that!'

Some cadets laughed. That made Ryan even more mad. He started pounding the boy's face with his fists, but it didn't have the desired effect.

The lad made no effort to stop him. The harder Ryan hit him, the more he seemed to enjoy it. 'Come on,' he yelled. 'I almost felt that one!'

'Ryan, STOP!' shouted Lee, trying to grab hold of Ryan's arms. But Ryan shook him off. He threw himself at the older cadet and wrestled him to the floor.

It was pointless. The boy fought him off with ease. He grabbed Ryan's arm and twisted it, before placing his knee on Ryan's back and holding his face against the cold tiles.

'So you want to play, do you?' he asked. He picked up a piece of toast covered in jam and rammed it in Ryan's hair, rubbing it back and forth for maximum effect. Satisfied at the result, the boy let go, stood up and dusted himself off.

He stood over Ryan, his face red and blotchy, blood streaming from his nose. 'I suggest you learn some respect, new boy,' he spat. 'I hope you enjoyed our little fight, because you're gonna pay dearly for what you did to my face.' He aimed a kick at Ryan's stomach, making him cough and retch. 'And just so you know,' the boy added, 'in future, I won't let you hit me like that.'

The lad walked away and the small crowd slowly dispersed.

'Who was that?' Ryan asked Lee, trying to wipe jam out of his hair.

'That's James Sarrell. You don't mess with him.'

'Why did he let me hit him? Why didn't he try to defend himself?'

'No idea,' admitted Lee, 'but you shouldn't have done it. He won't leave you alone now. He's gonna make your life a total misery.'

'Great,' said Ryan. 'That's just great.'

It didn't matter. None of it mattered. He was seeing his parents soon and then he'd get to leave this hell-hole of a school.

6. AIR

The first lesson did nothing to change Ryan's mind about wanting to leave. He was in an old-fashioned classroom that looked like it belonged in the last century. The students sat at rows of ancient wooden desks, ink wells in the top right corner.

The lesson was 'Global Economics' and the teacher, Mrs Tracey, was talking about subjects which were way over Ryan's head. He struggled to stay awake as she droned on.

'What I want each of you to do,' she concluded, 'is to write a short essay outlining at least three strategies that can be used to stabilise the economy during the initial stages of a stock market crash. There will be no need to talk.'

The students started writing. Time dragged by as Ryan sat there feeling awkward. Mrs Tracey didn't seem to notice.

Eventually, to his relief, a loud beep marked the end of the lesson and they were all dismissed. The students left their papers in a pile on the front desk as they exited the room. Ryan followed Lee out. 'That was the worst hour of my life,' he complained. 'This school is the pits.'

Instead of being offended, Lee grinned at him.

'See if you think that after the next lesson.'

They made their way outside, following a path that hugged the school building. Ryan could hear a helicopter nearby. As they turned the corner, he was surprised to see there were six army choppers on the school sports field. The students were making their way towards them.

'Are we going somewhere?' he asked.

'Not exactly,' said Lee. 'This is our flying lesson.'

Ryan was speechless, wondering if Lee meant what he said. He followed him to one of the helicopters. Climbing inside, he was handed a helmet and strapped in.

A pilot sat at the controls, dressed in full army combats. One other student was there; a black girl who introduced herself as Ayana.

'Ok, cadets, you all set?' asked the pilot. The voice was metallic through the comms system.

'Affirmative,' said Lee.

There was a sudden lurch as the helicopter rose into the air.

The pilot talked them through each manoeuvre. Lee was taking a close interest but Ryan was too dumbstruck to pay any attention. Before yesterday he'd never been in a helicopter before. Now it was becoming a regular occurrence.

After they had been airborne for a few minutes, the pilot turned to Lee. 'Cadet, it's your turn. The exercise starts in one minute.'

'Yes, sir.' Lee leaned forward to take the controls.

'Handing over in three, two, one... she's all yours,

cadet.'

There was no noticeable change as Lee took over. He knew what he was doing.

'Right, let's get ourselves a target!' he said.

'Enemy located at fifteen degrees,' reported Ayana, checking a screen in front of her.

Lee banked to the right. Flipping a few switches and engaging the onboard computer, he eased the craft until the cross-hairs hovered over another helicopter. 'Die, losers!' he shouted, as he pressed the trigger. A confirmation appeared on the screen: TARGET ELIMINATED.

'That's one down,' muttered Lee. 'Now, where are the others?'

'Careful. There's one above us!' warned Ayana. 'It's close!'

Lee cursed, and the chopper lurched as he veered away from the enemy aircraft. Ryan's stomach became queasy as they banked left, then right. He no longer had any clue where the ground was. Lee wasn't having a lot of luck in his evasive movements. The craft rose sharply, then dipped.

The ground filled the view in front of them and Ryan could make out tiny buildings and roads below. He tried not to think about how high they must be or how many seconds it would take to fall that kind of distance.

I'm not afraid of heights, Ryan reminded himself.

Which was good, because there was another sudden change of course and the ground disappeared—all was blue sky and distant clouds. It was worse than a rollercoaster.

Ryan held tight to his seat, his face white. Bile rose in his throat and he forced himself to swallow. He was regretting having the full cooked breakfast.

Another shout went up from Ayana—they were under attack. More frantic manoeuvres, a sudden dive, then a crazy spin. And then it happened, before Ryan could stop it.

He puked.

When he opened his eyes he groaned as he realised he had thrown up all over himself, the seat, and Ayana. Vomit was everywhere.

'Awww,' moaned Ayana, 'that's gross!'

Lee was still focused on scoring points, and he'd got the other helicopter in his sights. Squeezing the trigger, he gave off a whoop as he hit his next target.

But now the smell of sick was overpowering. With the sudden movements, it was a fatal combination. Ryan gagged and threw up again, keeping his head down between his knees, the vomit ending up mostly on the floor. As the chopper banked left and right, it sloshed from one side of the cockpit to the other.

'Seriously?' shouted Ayana, lifting her boots. 'Could you stop doing that?'

'Sorry,' gagged Ryan, sounding pathetic. 'I'm doing my best. I can't help it!'

'Do what you can, Ryan,' said Lee, focusing on his next target. 'I've got three more to go!'

'I'm afraid not, cadet,' said the pilot, glancing back. 'We're going to abort. I'm taking the controls back in three, two, one...'

Landing the helicopter seemed to take an age. Ryan felt like a complete idiot. When they settled back onto the sports field, he clambered out, fell to his knees and threw up again, getting the last of it out of his system. His legs were shaky, and he gripped the grass between his fingers, clinging to it for reassurance.

'Unlucky, son,' the pilot said to Lee as they exited the craft. 'You were doing well out there. Better luck next time.'

'Thank you, sir.' Lee walked over to Ryan and placed a hand on his shoulder. 'You doing ok?' he asked.

'Yeah, sorry,' said Ryan, coughing. 'You really know how to fly!'

'Yeah, I love it,' said Lee. 'I never got the chance before I came to Devonmoor.'

'I didn't mean to ruin your game. Was the score important?'

Lee didn't respond for a moment. 'No, not that important. Let's get you cleaned up.'

Ryan glanced down at his clothes.

'Good idea.'

7. CONTROL

They didn't have to walk far to get to a small rectangular block sat at the edge of the field. Inside was an empty changing room with dark-green walls, high windows and long benches. It smelt of dirt and sweat, and looked like it hadn't been cleaned in months.

A white tiled area led to a row of communal showers. Ryan didn't hang around. He stripped off and stepped in. When he turned the dial, the water was freezing and didn't seem to get any warmer, but he needed to get clean so he forced himself under. Lee disappeared and came back with a towel and clean uniform.

'I owe you so badly,' acknowledged Ryan, taking the stuff and feeling a little awkward as he dried himself.

'How did you get that?' asked Lee, seeing a deep scar running across Ryan's back.

'Car accident,' said Ryan. 'A few years ago. It was pretty serious.' He started pulling on the clothes.

Lee glanced at the clock above the door. 'Hurry,' he urged Ryan. 'Break-time is almost over.'

'So what's the next lesson? Scuba diving? Bungee jumping?' Ryan meant it as a joke, but it wouldn't have surprised him if they were on the timetable.

Lee smiled in a good-natured way. 'Devonmoor takes a bit of getting used to,' he admitted, 'but no, we have emotional intelligence next.' He must have noticed the bewildered look on Ryan's face. 'It's kind of understanding how to read other people's expressions and control your own emotions and stuff.'

'Well, it sounds better than global economics.' Ryan stuffed his feet in the heavy boots. 'Let's go.'

As they jogged back to the main building, Lee tried to explain which lessons were good and which weren't so great. The corridors were quiet, and he seemed flustered as they approached a classroom in the newer part of the building. He spoke in a hushed whisper. 'We're late. Don't say anything unless you have to and I'll try to cover for us. Dr Torren is a little eccentric, but he's alright.'

As they walked in, Ryan could see what Lee meant. Dr Torren was wearing a pin-striped suit and waistcoat, looking much smarter than any teacher Ryan had ever seen. His face was sharp and angular, with a tiny triangle of a beard and piercing blue eyes. He looked like a TV magician.

'Ah, Cadet Young,' he said, 'how good of you to join us.' He turned his attention to Ryan. 'And this must be our newest acquisition.'

'Sorry we're late sir,' said Lee. 'I had to, err, show Cadet Jacobs around.'

Dr Torren addressed the other students, sat in a giant 'U' shape around the room. 'Well class, what do you think? What can we tell from the cadet's apology?'

A few hands went up, and the teacher pointed at a girl.

'He's telling the truth, but he's leaving out significant details,' she said.

'Yes, yes,' the teacher responded, 'but we can do better than that. Adams?'

'Cadet Young is protective of the new cadet. He's shielding him from the room. He doesn't want him to be embarrassed or to get into trouble.'

Ryan hadn't realised this, but sure enough, Lee was using his body to block him from everyone else. Lee stepped aside now it had been pointed out.

'Getting better,' said the teacher. 'Now build on it. Cadet Jeet?' He nodded to an Asian boy.

'The new cadet has wet hair and his boots haven't been tied properly. He dressed in a hurry like he's come straight from the showers.'

'Good, good,' the teacher seemed pleased. 'Cadet Young has been in the shower block all break-time with his new friend and that is what he didn't want to say.'

Some students smirked. Ryan was embarrassed, but for once he was too out of his comfort zone to say anything.

'Take your seats, cadets,' said the teacher, more kindly than Ryan expected. They both sat down, glad that the public inquisition was over.

Dr Torren turned to face the class. 'Today we'll be looking at one of the most powerful weapons any person can wield: that of suggestion,' he said. 'It allows us to influence or control people without them knowing. With suggestion on your side, you can change the way people behave and often prevent the need for a fight.'

A well-built lad at the back of the room let out a snort and leaned back on his chair.

'It seems that Cadet Hayes may disagree. Am I correct?' Rather than appearing annoyed, the teacher looked pleased.

'Well, sir, I'd rather have a gun than the power of suggestion any day,' admitted Hayes. From their reactions, a couple of others seemed to agree.

'Ok, come up here,' said Dr Torren. 'Let's demonstrate these forces at work.'

Hayes scraped his chair as he stood up and sauntered to the front to stand next to Dr Torren. He was a big lad, that was for sure, the same height as the teacher.

'Have you ever wanted to hit me, Hayes?'

The cadet hesitated. His eyes narrowed.

'It's ok, it's not a trick question,' Dr Torren reassured him. 'You must have, at some point, wanted to punch me?'

'I thought about it, sir,' Hayes admitted, 'but I would never do it.'

'Well, in a few minutes time I will allow you to hit me as hard as you like.'

There was a sudden hush in the classroom and everyone sat up straighter.

'But I can't, sir; I'd be expelled,' said the cadet, a

little confused.

'Normally, yes, but this is not a normal situation,' continued Dr Torren. 'For the purposes of teaching I will ask you to punch me in the face and there will be no consequences. The entire class have witnessed me saying this, so you are quite safe. You will, in fact, only be following my instructions. Ok?'

'Yeah, sure,' said Hayes, his lip curling. 'If you want me to hit you, I'll hit you, sir.' He clearly thought Dr Torren was crazy, but he was also relishing the opportunity to assault a teacher.

'But first I want you to notice how you're feeling,' Dr Torren locked eyes with Hayes. 'Think about how much you weigh, compared to me. All that training in the gym, all of that muscle, must feel pretty good on your body. But as you focus on your legs, they seem heavy. They're like dead weights right now as you're standing there. It's difficult to move them, weighing as much as they do. The stronger they are, the more difficult it is, isn't that right? They're so heavy that they are stuck to the floor.'

'Err, what?' Hayes looked confused.

'Relax, Hayes. Can you do that for me? As you relax, that feeling you have in the lower part of your body is spreading upwards. It's like your whole body is turning to stone. You'd need to be really strong to resist it and the stronger you are, the more your body weighs, and the harder it is to move. By now you can't even feel your arms and legs. The invisible shell that surrounds your body is getting harder and harder. You are, in fact, unable to do anything, other than stand.'

It was true: Hayes appeared to be frozen to the spot. His hands gave a feeble twitch.

'Now,' said Dr Torren, clearing his throat, 'I believe we had a deal, Cadet Hayes. You may hit me.' The teacher moved towards the lad for effect, but Hayes didn't budge. 'Not in the mood? I'm afraid my offer will expire in ten seconds.' Dr Torren laughed and turned to address the class. 'As I was saying, suggestion is incredibly powerful and you would be wise not to underestimate its effects...'

He carried on teaching, leaving Hayes standing at the front for the rest of the lesson. The cadet remained motionless for at least forty minutes. As the lesson ended, Dr Torren told him he could now move again and Hayes came back to life, looking exhausted.

'Never mess with Dr Torren,' Lee whispered to Ryan as they left the classroom. 'He can persuade anyone to do anything. It's scary.'

'I can believe it,' Ryan agreed, a shiver running down his spine. It freaked him out to see a kid being controlled like that. Surely Dr Torren couldn't do that to him? It didn't bear thinking about. 'Doesn't it bother you, knowing a teacher has that much power?'

'Not really,' replied Lee. 'Dr Torren's alright. He's one of the better teachers.'

What on earth are the worst teachers like? thought Ryan, glad that he wouldn't be staying long enough to find out. 'So, what happens now?' he asked. 'Another lesson?'

The corridor was buzzing with people and Lee led Ryan towards a staircase. They descended into a basement.

'Yep, but this one's pretty good,' said Lee, with that interminable optimism that was both endearing and annoying. 'You'll like this.'

'Yeah? What is it?'

'Computing.'

For once, thought Ryan, Lee was probably right.

8. SHOCK

They walked into the most impressive computer room that Ryan had ever seen.

A haphazard arrangement of shiny steel desks filled the space. Computers and other complicated-looking devices packed the surfaces, connected with twisted cables. Several gigantic screens dominated the front of the room, branching out from the teacher's desk. A mainframe sat next to it: a cube of electronics complete with circuit boards, screens and blinking LEDs. At the back was a steel walkway, two metres high, also full of machines.

The room was dark—there were no windows at all—and the subdued blue spotlights added to the futuristic atmosphere; they gleamed and reflected off the metal surfaces, making it appear like the interior of a spaceship.

Bustling around at the front was Mr Davids, the guy that Ryan had met in the helicopter. He wore a lab coat over the same Hawaiian shirt. His face lit up when he saw Ryan.

'Aha, you're here, at last!' His general enthusiasm flowed into every one of his words. 'Erm, Ryan isn't it?'

'Yes, sir,' responded Ryan. 'We met last night.'

'Of course. Take a seat, take a seat!' The excited teacher ushered him to a desk near the front. Lee had slipped to his usual place further back.

'Right, class, we have been working on system security this term,' he began. 'Well today we have a new student with us who is interested in this topic, yes?'

Ryan felt awkward being singled out. The last thing he wanted was to draw attention to himself. This was turning into a really bad day. He nodded, hoping it would satisfy Mr Davids so he would move on.

'Ryan here hacked into the army computer system last night,' the teacher explained, 'so he is something of an expert.'

'Then how come he got caught?'

Ryan wasn't sure who said it, but several people laughed. Blood rushed to his cheeks.

'Unfortunately for Ryan, his little diversions were not enough to stop us from tracking him in the end. And that leads me on to today's topic: we will examine different tactics hackers use in order to break into systems, and how we can overcome them...'

From here, Mr Davids warmed to his subject and Ryan stopped feeling self-conscious as the teacher spoke of ways that systems could be compromised. He learned so much in the next half hour that his head was buzzing. He wanted to talk to the teacher one-on-one, to explore the subject in greater depth.

He never got the opportunity. A female prefect arrived to take him out of the lesson.

'Where are we going?' he asked, as they headed

down the corridor.

'To Lady Devonmoor's office. Your parents are here.'

About time, thought Ryan, *I can get this mess sorted out*.

'I'm Ryan by the way.'

'Yes, I know. They sent me to fetch you, remember?' The girl gave him a withering look as if she didn't want to speak to him.

Well screw you, he thought to himself.

They walked on in silence.

Ryan let out a gasp of relief when he entered the room. There, sitting on the couch, were his mum and dad. He ran towards them and they stood up and embraced him. 'Mum, Dad, I'm sorry...' he said.

'It's ok,' said his mum, running her hand through his hair. 'You gave us quite a shock, but I think we're going to be able to sort it out.'

Ryan looked at his dad and was surprised to see that he wasn't angry. He looked calm—unusually calm in fact.

'You've really crossed the line this time, haven't you?' he said. This was a guy who would normally blow his fuse if Ryan so much as left his football boots in the hallway.

'I guess so,' admitted Ryan, confused by the gentle manner. Something wasn't right.

'Shall we get started?' The head-teacher ushered everyone to their seats.

Ryan sat between his parents on the large sofa while Lady Devonmoor settled In an armchair. Dr

Torren was there, looking relaxed and sipping a cup of tea. He glanced up at Ryan but said nothing.

'I've been apprising your parents of the current situation,' said the head-teacher, 'and you are very lucky. They have agreed to let you stay at the academy, if the Board permits it of course.'

'What? They said what?' He looked at his parents, sure that the old lady must have misunderstood.

'Don't be upset, Ryan,' urged his mum. 'It's ok. We've talked it through and this seems to be for the best.'

'Without even asking me?' Ryan jumped to his feet and turned to his father. 'Dad! Tell her!' Whatever support he was expecting didn't materialise.

'The truth is, Ryan, it's a real opportunity,' he said. 'If you pass the interview, they'll offer you a full scholarship.'

'But I don't want a scholarship! I don't want to stay here! Don't you care what I think?'

His father looked him in the eye. 'If you don't stay here, then Lady Devonmoor says the army will charge you with an act of terrorism. We could fight it legally but it's too risky.' He had made his mind up. 'All things considered, they're letting you off pretty lightly. Besides, given the stunt you pulled last night, maybe a bit of discipline is just what you need.'

Ryan slumped back on the sofa, his head in his hands. 'You *can't* be serious!'

If he was honest, his own feelings were a little confused. He hated how strict the place was, but this was a school where they taught you to fly helicopters, and he could learn so much from Mr Davids. That might be worth sticking around for.

'You'll get to come home in the holidays,' his mum said, trying to soften the blow.

'You mean I can't even see you at weekends?'

'It's too far. Besides, we're told that the school has a very full extracurricular programme.'

There were so many questions, Ryan didn't know where to start. 'What about all my stuff? My computer? My phone? And football?'

'As I've told your parents this afternoon, Ryan,' said Lady Devonmoor, 'we don't allow students any private property here. We will provide everything you need.'

Ryan thought of the sparse dorm room with nothing in it but beds and wardrobes. He felt sick.

'And there will be plenty of opportunity for sports and other activities,' added Dr Torren. Ryan didn't like the way he said it.

'I need my clothes at least,' he pleaded, realising he sounded pathetic.

'At Devonmoor our students wear uniform *all* the time,' replied Dr Torren, enjoying the look of horror spreading over Ryan's face. 'So, I hope you like grey?'

'This gets worse and worse,' muttered Ryan. 'You can't make me do this.' He was wasting his breath.

'I think you can say goodbye to your parents now, Ryan,' said Lady Devonmoor. 'There are quite a few forms they need to sign before they leave.'

'Yes, of course,' said his dad. 'Thank you.'

'Let's hope the Board allow Ryan to stay,' she replied, standing up. 'I'll inform you of their decision later this afternoon.'

Ryan's mum gave him a peck on the cheek. 'Try not to get in any trouble. We'll come to fetch you at the end of term. I'm sure you can cope until then.'

'But that's weeks away!'

She gave him an apologetic look. 'It'll fly by, you'll see.'

As they made their way out, Ryan wanted to throw up. His parents were leaving him. He wanted to shake them, to shout, to scream, but he was too proud and angry to do it. So he did nothing: just sat on the sofa as they said their goodbyes.

He'd never thought he'd have to stay here. He'd assumed his parents would get him out of trouble, like they always did. He had known, *known*, that they would never allow him to stay at a place like this.

Dr Torren sipped his tea. 'That's right, Jacobs, don't fight it.'

'You?' said Ryan, suddenly realising. 'You hypnotised them?'

'Not quite. There's no need to be so dramatic,' replied the teacher. 'I might have helped to persuade them, but they weren't objectionable. They *may* have wanted it this way. You'll thank me later.'

Ryan was speechless. He tried to work through the storm of emotions that were playing out in his head. There was anger, that was for sure, but also excitement buried down there. And confusion, lots of confusion.

He pulled at the collar of his jacket, realising that he was going to be wearing this uniform for way longer than he had expected. It was hot and tight, threatening to steal his identity; the dark grey material sucking the colour out of his life, the thick socks bunched around his ankles like heavy chains.

Lady Devonmoor came back into the room and sat down. 'Now, dear, we need to talk.'

'I think he's a little angry,' mused Dr Torren. 'I'm not sure how much he wants to be here. He's not in the mood to co-operate.'

'Too right I'm not!' Ryan stood up. It freaked him out that he was being controlled, forced to remain there against his will.

Dr Torren leaned forward, looking Ryan in the eye. 'Jacobs, you need to trust us...' he began, but Ryan cut him off.

'Let me guess, you're going to hypnotise me as well!'

'No, not at all,' Dr Torren said. 'That wouldn't accomplish anything. Why don't you listen for a moment and if you want to have a hissy fit, then you can have it *after* we've given you the facts.'

Annoyed as he was, Ryan figured he had nowhere to go and having a tantrum wasn't the wisest course of action. He clenched his fists and tried to calm down.

'Dr Torren is not evil, Ryan,' soothed Lady Devonmoor. 'He simply ensured that your parents let you stay. As I explained earlier, it's important that we have you at this school. Talent like yours needs to be nurtured.'

Ryan glared at them both.

'Listen,' continued the head-teacher, 'this afternoon the School Board will meet to discuss your admission. You will be interviewed, and only if they agree to let you in will you become a student here.'

A glimmer of hope appeared in Ryan's eyes. 'So if I mess up the interview then I get to go home?'

'No, Jacobs,' said Dr Torren, 'if the Board reject you then you are released back into military custody. You're a security risk, so the army want to charge you and lock you up in a secure unit. They have a place called Blackfell where they keep dangerous juveniles like you.'

Ryan wasn't sure whether he could trust the information they were giving him. It all seemed too incredible, too unreal. 'Surely that's not legal,' he objected. 'I'm not dangerous. I'm only thirteen.'

'A thirteen-year-old who can hack into the Ministry of Defence mainframe.' Dr Torren raised his eyebrows. 'Trust me, they'll find a way to keep you locked up, and Blackfell makes this place look like a holiday camp.'

Ryan shook his head. 'There must be some chance they wouldn't send me there? They might drop the charges and let me go home?'

'Possibly,' said Dr Torren, stroking his beard, 'but I imagine that would only happen on the condition that you didn't use any technology more advanced than a toaster until you were at least eighteen. You wouldn't be allowed near a computer.'

No, this couldn't be happening.

Ryan didn't want to imagine what that would be like. His life would be over. That was almost worse than the threat of Blackfell.

He rubbed his legs and looked into the eyes of both of the adults. They seemed genuine.

'Fine,' he conceded. 'Let's assume I want to stay. How do I pass this interview?'

The two teachers looked at each other.

'Well, Jacobs,' said Dr Torren, standing up. 'I hope you're ready for an intense lesson on how to impress the Board.'

9. THERAPY

Dr Torren's room was an odd place. A huge floor-to-ceiling window overlooked the grounds, but all the other walls were painted black. It was empty except for two comfortable black leather chairs. Ryan wasn't sure whether the overall effect was calming or creepy. He sat in one chair and Dr Torren sat across from him in his pristine suit.

'Is this like therapy?' Ryan asked, curious about the set-up.

Dr Torren laughed. 'I'm able to conduct therapy if you need it?'

'No.' Ryan stared at the wall.

'I can see you're still angry with me,' Dr Torren observed. 'We'd better deal with that first or we won't accomplish anything before the Board meets. What's the problem?'

'What do you think! You hypnotised my parents to keep me here!'

'I see.' Dr Torren nodded, unfazed. 'But we told your parents the truth. All I did was help them accept the facts. I ensured your father was calm enough to think clearly.'

'What right do you have to control him? To make him do what you want?' Ryan stood up and started pacing.

'It's a good question,' acknowledged Dr Torren, 'and one that I could also ask you.'

Ryan paused. 'What do you mean?'

'In June you stole your dad's credit card and used it to buy some expensive computer hardware. Correct?' Ryan said nothing so Dr Torren continued. 'When your dad found out, he was furious. He took your computer away. What did you do?'

Ryan sat back down on the chair, his cheeks burning. He looked away from the teacher. 'It sounds like you already know,' he said. 'I wrecked my room.'

'And?' Dr Torren wasn't going to let him off that easily.

'I refused to go to school. I threatened to smash up his car.' It wasn't easy admitting that he'd been a spoilt brat but Dr Torren had obviously got the full story from his parents.

'Your parents talked it all out with you, and you settled down again, right?'

'Yeah, it was all good. It was a normal family argument.'

'But you got your computer back as part of the deal?' Dr Torren leaned forward, watching Ryan.

'Yeah, so what?'

'So here's what I think. I think you got what you wanted, and that you always slip out of the consequences of the actions you take. As far as you're concerned, the rules don't apply to you.'

'That's not true!' objected Ryan.

'But it is,' countered Dr Torren. 'What about the

65

money you siphoned off several bank accounts in the last few months? What gives you the right to do that?'

Ryan looked away. No-one had come close to figuring that out until now. He'd been careful.

'You think you're exempt from the rules, because you are Ryan Jacobs, you are special. In fact, you couldn't even follow the rules if you wanted to. Am I right?'

That accusation hurt. It really hurt. Anger bubbled up inside him. Dr Torren didn't know about his past. He had no idea what Ryan had been through.

'You manipulate your parents all the time,' carried on the doctor, 'and your teachers, and even your friends.'

'You don't know me!' shouted Ryan.

'The thing is, Jacobs,' smiled the teacher, 'I do know you, slouching there in the chair like you own the place with your stylish haircut and your rich daddy. You think the world owes you something, and that you can do whatever you like. I also know that you can't follow the rules.'

'Who says I can't follow the rules?' Ryan was furious that he was being judged by someone he'd just met.

'Well let's find out,' said Dr Torren. 'That should be "Who says I can't follow the rules, *sir*?"'

Ryan felt trapped. 'Who says I can't follow the rules, *sir*?' he repeated back, emphasising the 'sir' with a particular vehemence.

Dr Torren laughed. 'Look, Jacobs. I know what you're like and you're proving it. You're spoilt, you're angry and you're rebellious. But you're also clever. We can work on the other stuff over time. Right now, we need to get you through this Board meeting, and for that you need to work with me, even if you hate me. Do you understand?'

'Yeah,' said Ryan. 'I understand, *sir.*'

'Good,' said Dr Torren. 'Let's try that again, but this time without any sarcasm. Remember what's at stake here. Do you want to be able to carry on using computers? Isn't that worth swallowing your pride for?'

Ryan fidgeted in his seat. 'Ok,' he said, watching his tone. 'I understand, sir.'

'That's better,' Dr Torren leaned back in his chair. 'Now, stand to attention.'

Ryan looked at him, checking he was serious. Then, he stood up, letting his arms drop to his sides.

'When you enter the room,' said Dr Torren, 'how you do so will be critical. You'll need to march in there and stand to attention, pretty much how you're standing now, but straighten your back a little, face forward. Always keep your face forward. Don't look around. Don't slouch or move your arms...'

Ryan spent the next hour learning what seemed to be the finer points of military etiquette: how to march, how to salute, how to stand at ease. Dr Torren also talked him through the overall impression he wanted to give, the things he mustn't do under any circumstances. As the session progressed, he relaxed a little, sensing that in some bizarre way, Dr Torren was on his side. If nothing else, he was a patient teacher.

'If you do what I've told you,' he said, 'then you stand the best possible chance of being a given a place at the academy. The colonel will try to make you angry. He'll try to break you. He wants to show the Board that you don't belong here, and if you argue, or lose your temper, or whine then they will agree with him. Don't give him the satisfaction, ok?'

'Yes, sir,' responded Ryan.

And this time there wasn't a hint of defiance. If they wanted to see the perfect obedient cadet, he would play the part.

He needed to prove Dr Torren wrong: to show him he could follow the rules when he wanted. If he was honest, he also needed to prove that to himself.

10. BOARDROOM

After a brief lunch, Ryan was summoned to the boardroom. It was an intimidating place. Fifteen adults sat like a courtroom jury, behind a line of polished desks. He marched to the centre of the room and stood to attention, staring straight ahead.

'You must be Ryan Jacobs?' asked a dark-haired woman. She looked pretty officious and Ryan guessed she was in charge of proceedings.

'Yes ma'am,' he replied. The formality of his response surprised him.

'You understand we are here to discuss your nomination to be a cadet at this academy?'

'Yes ma'am.'

'Good. At ease, cadet.'

Ryan allowed himself to loosen up a little, moving his hands behind his back and relaxing his posture.

An older gentlemen shuffled the papers in front of him and looked at Ryan over the top of his spectacles. 'The Board has heard that you were brought to this school following a criminal act. You tried to hack into the Ministry of Defence. Is this true?'

'Yes, sir.'

'So you are a criminal by your own admission?'

Ryan flinched a little at the use of the word

'criminal' but there was no point denying it. 'Yes, sir. I am.'

'Do you have anything to say in your defence?' asked the man, assessing Ryan carefully, as he might have examined a piece of antique furniture.

'Yes, sir,' said Ryan. 'I realise what I did was wrong, but I didn't mean any harm. I just wanted the challenge. I'd like to apologise for the inconvenience I caused.'

Out of the corner of his eye he could see the colonel. As Ryan made his apology, the colonel started to clap very slowly.

'Well, well,' he said, standing up. 'Aren't you an angel all of a sudden? Good show. Well done.' He walked around the desks to stand near Ryan, addressing the panel as he did so. 'Are you going to believe this act? This boy knows exactly what he's doing. It's not like he made a one-off mistake; the army have been aware of his activity for months. Do you think that he's going to change just because he's been brought here? A rebel like him will contaminate this academy and put the entire Project at risk.'

Ryan wanted to respond, but Dr Torren had told him not to say anything unless he was asked.

'Dr Fleur, you've had time to assess the boy?' asked the woman in charge.

'I carried out an obedience test on arrival,' Dr Fleur replied. 'I'm afraid to say that he failed, rather spectacularly in fact. The moment I left the room he broke the rules, as we expected he would.'

It was all a test, thought Ryan. No wonder they'd

70

been stupid enough to leave him alone on the running machine. They wanted to see whether he'd try to escape.

'What conclusions did you draw?'

Dr Fleur cleared her throat. 'Well, he's the only cadet we've ever had that failed. Combined with the other information we've gathered on Jacobs, I would have to say that he has clear signs of Oppositional Defiant Disorder. In short, he has serious issues with authority.'

The man with spectacles looked up. 'Have we ever had any other cadets at the academy with that diagnosis?'

'Only one,' Dr Fleur said with meaning. 'Several years ago, before we introduced the obedience test. I think we all know what happened there.' A murmur broke out in the room and Ryan could see the colonel smirking at him, as if his fate was sealed. He started to sweat. This wasn't looking good.

'Mr Davids,' said the chairperson, cutting across the noise. 'You asked to be here to present your case?'

Ryan hadn't realised the computer teacher was there.

'Yes, thank you, yes, err, well, the Project needs people with the skills that Ryan has. He shows remarkable talent in his computing knowledge, yes? More than any cadet we have, in fact. Many of our students are capable programmers but they are too compliant to have built up these kinds of hacking skills.'

'But surely you can train them in that area?' demanded the chairperson. 'They're all bright kids after all!'

'It's not that easy,' explained Mr Davids. 'Hacking is not just a skill; it's a mindset, a mentality. It needs people who can take risks and break rules. As we've already heard, Ryan's brain works differently to most in that regard. It's only *because* of that is he able to bring a unique perspective.'

The old guy with spectacles peered at the teacher with interest. 'You make a fascinating point, Mr Davids,' he said. 'New solutions require new paradigms. Sometimes that means we have to break old rules or be willing to question the most sacred traditions. But our other cadets are quite capable of challenging the accepted wisdom in their fields without doing anything illegal.'

'That is true, sir,' said Mr Davids, 'but I would argue that those who questioned the system and broke the rules have always made the most remarkable computing breakthroughs. I believe that with Ryan on board the Project would be much more likely to thrive.'

'Assuming he was working *for* us,' interjected the colonel, 'but what if he rebels or sells out to the other side? Dr Fleur has already reminded us of the last student we took a risk on. We can't afford for that to happen again.'

'Colonel Keller,' said the chairperson, 'you seem to have very strong views about this boy. Other than his love of hacking, do you have any reason to believe this boy will be a bad influence at the academy?'

'Yes, I do. If the Board will permit me to call a witness?'

'Go ahead, Colonel.'

The door opened and Ryan heard someone walking in. He wanted to turn to see who it was, but he had been told by Dr Torren to always face the front. As the footsteps drew closer, he glimpsed the new arrival through his peripheral vision. It was the tall cadet with the shaved head; the one he had fought at breakfast.

'What is your name, cadet?' asked the colonel.

'Sarrell. James Sarrell, sir,' responded the cadet sharply.

'At ease,' continued Colonel Keller. 'Could you explain what happened to your face?'

'Yes, sir,' said Sarrell. 'I went over to introduce myself to Jacobs here and he flung himself at me, throwing punches. He was wild.'

'Did you do or say anything that might explain his behaviour?'

'No, sir,' lied Sarrell. 'I was just being friendly.'

The chairperson scribbled a few notes on her paper, before looking up. 'Did you start a fight with cadet Sarrell this morning?' she asked Ryan.

Ryan wanted to argue his side: Sarrell had poured his drink over him! He'd started it! But it was true that Ryan had thrown the first punch.

Don't get angry, Dr Torren's words came back to him. *Accept responsibility. Apologise. Drop your eyes.*

'Yes, ma'am,' said Ryan. He turned to Cadet Sarrell. 'I'm sorry.'

It hurt Ryan to apologise to his new enemy, but it was worth it to see the colonel's response. He glared at Ryan, frustrated.

Ryan also noticed with satisfaction that Sarrell's face was cut and bruised from the fight. It might have been a set-up, but at least he had caused him pain.

The woman in charge cleared her throat. 'You may leave now, Sarrell,' she said. 'Thank you.'

As the older lad left, the Board members started muttering to one another in subdued tones.

'It seems you lack a little discipline,' the elderly man commented, as people quietened down. 'Would you agree?'

'Yes, sir,' Ryan responded, 'But I'm willing to change. That's why I want to stay. I'll learn. I'll do whatever it takes.'

'You realise that the rules here are incredibly strict?'

'Yes, sir. I can handle it.'

'Hmmm.' The man didn't seem convinced.

'Does anyone have any additional questions for the cadet?' asked the chairperson.

No-one did, and they asked Ryan to leave. He sat in the grand entrance hall while the Board continued their discussion. He thought about all the things he should have said. Surely he should have stood up for himself and told them what had happened in the canteen?

After what seemed like an age, he heard the scraping of chairs and he stood to attention. The door to the boardroom opened, and the colonel walked over to him.

'Good try, Jacobs,' he sneered. 'You almost persuaded them to let you stay, but they saw through your little act.'

Ryan's heart sank. He'd failed.

'Not got anything to say, Jacobs?' asked the colonel. 'I'm surprised. There's no point pretending to be the good little cadet any longer.'

Ryan looked at him, thinking how good it would feel to punch him in the face, but to his surprise he was more disappointed than angry. 'What happens now?'

'Now, Jacobs? Now the army get you back. You'll go to trial, and if there's any justice, you'll end up at a nice little place called Blackfell.'

'Blackfell?' Ryan gulped. 'What's it like?'

'Trust me,' said the colonel, giving an evil grin. 'You don't want to know. But you're about to find out.'

11. VOMIT

As the colonel walked off, Ryan looked around, a sense of panic rising within him. The entrance hall was empty. Maybe he should try to escape again? What did he have to lose? This might be his last chance.

He was about to make a break for it, when the other Board members emerged in clusters of two and three. Most of them walked past him, but Lady Devonmoor stopped.

'Well, Cadet Jacobs,' she said with a warm smile. 'Congratulations! You are now officially a student of Devonmoor Academy.'

'What?' asked Ryan, wondering if he'd misheard. 'How? The colonel said that I'd failed.'

'Ah. Probably one of his little tests,' replied the head-teacher.

Ryan felt a huge sense of relief that he wasn't being taken to Blackfell after all, but he also realised how close he'd already come to losing his chance at Devonmoor. He'd underestimated the colonel. The man would even lie to his face in order to get Ryan into trouble. He'd been hoping that Ryan would do something stupid, like hit him or make a run for it. And truth be told, Ryan had almost done exactly that.

'It won't surprise you that Colonel Keller does not agree with the decision,' Lady Devonmoor carried on. 'He's sure that you'll lead the other cadets astray and compromise the Project.'

'I won't!'

'I know, dear.' She put her hand on his shoulder and looked at him. 'But don't expect him to go easy on you. Try to avoid upsetting him. He's looking for any excuse to have you expelled.'

'Yes, ma'am, I'll try,' he said. Then his curiosity got the better of him. 'Why does he hate me so much?'

Lady Devonmoor paused, as if she wasn't sure whether she should answer. 'We had a student a bit like you in the past,' she said, softly. 'He was into hacking and had difficulty following the rules. It didn't end well. That's partly why we have to keep security here so tight.'

'Right.'

'So, don't go hacking into any other systems. Not unless you have Mr David's permission. That's just the kind of thing Colonel Keller would need to have you sent to Blackfell.'

'Sure, ma'am,' said Ryan. 'I'll keep clear of that. I promise.'

And he was serious.

He had no intention of making that mistake again.

***

Ryan's relief soon disappeared as he realised how tough his new life was going to be. A few hours after his conversation with Lady Devonmoor, he was kneeling inside a military helicopter with a bucket and a stiff brush. He was wearing a dark-blue boiler suit and rubber gloves while he cleaned the sick out of the vehicle's interior. The smell was overpowering: a mixture of antiseptic, bleach and semi-dried vomit.

He wasn't the only one involved. To his horror, they had also called the rest of the lads in his dormitory out to assist him. He'd tried to object, but to no avail.

'It's what happens here, mate,' explained Lee, as he wiped the helicopter dials with a damp cloth. 'If anyone gets into trouble then everyone in their dorm shares the consequences.'

'But that's not fair!'

'Probably not, but it works.'

Lee had tried to appear cheerful as they carried out the grim task, acting as if he enjoyed cleaning up the contents of Ryan's stomach. The other lads were less positive, but to be fair, they didn't complain.

'You realise you owe us big?' Jael said, when he had seen the inside of the helicopter.

'Yeah,' Kev added. 'Next time you have flying lessons, don't eat, ok?'

'No talking.' The pilot from earlier was supervising them. 'I want this bird to gleam when you've finished. If I find you've missed any part of it, then you'll be back to do it again.'

They had been at it for over half an hour when the colonel arrived.

'Well, well,' he said. 'I see they've found a use for

you after all, Jacobs. Maybe it's not such a bad thing that they let you stay. I'm sure going to enjoy having you here.'

Ryan furiously scrubbed the floor of the helicopter. *Don't get angry,* he told himself, *stay calm.*

'Thank you, sir.'

The colonel turned to Lee, Jael and Kev. 'When you've finished, show Jacobs around the place and explain the rules to him. From now on, he's your responsibility.' He shook his head in mock sympathy. 'I sure feel sorry for you boys. He's only been here a day and you're already cleaning up his mess! God knows how much trouble he'll cause.'

'Yes, sir,' Kev responded, his tone neutral.

Ryan looked up, anticipating more abuse, as the colonel towered over him.

'By the way, Jacobs,' he said, 'I never got to say: welcome to Devonmoor.' He kicked over the bucket, the contents pouring out onto the floor and swimming around Ryan's knees.

Ryan stood up and swore at the colonel, unable to hold it in any longer: 'What the hell! What's your problem? You're insane, you know that?'

Rather than being angry, the colonel gave an evil smile. 'Oh dear,' he said. 'Tut tut, Jacobs. You're not cut out for this whole discipline thing, are you? Get out.'

Ryan threw down the brush he was holding and clambered out of the helicopter, radiating contempt.

'Stand to attention!' ordered the colonel.

Ryan was sick of being ordered around. 'Or what?'

he demanded.

'Or you and your friends will clean the other five helicopters as well. How's that for a start?'

Ryan could see the concern on Lee's face. The colonel wasn't bluffing. He sighed and stood up straight.

The man stepped forward and spoke to Ryan in an icy tone. 'I don't know what kind of behaviour was acceptable at your old school, but things work differently here. You will learn to respect authority.'

'Yes, sir.' Ryan forced the words out, each one causing him pain.

'So here's how it's going to work. You're going to stand here while your friends finish clearing up your mess. If you move so much as an inch then both you and they will lose *all* of your free time this week.' He turned to the pilot. 'Let me know if the boy moves.'

'Yes, sir.'

And with that, the colonel strode off across the field, leaving Ryan standing like a statue in the dusk.

Don't let them manipulate you like this, Ryan thought to himself, furious the colonel had found a way to control him. But what could he do?

However much he wanted to rebel and storm off, he knew the colonel would carry out his threat, and the last thing Ryan wanted to do was to lose any chance of friendship with his room-mates.

Fortunately, the boys only took another twenty minutes to finish the job. It felt like an hour to Ryan.

'Ok, lads,' said the pilot. 'That's a job well done. You can go now.' He turned to Ryan. 'That includes you.'

All four of them trudged back to the changing rooms as the sky grew dark.

'I'm so sorry.' Ryan apologised, feeling helpless.

'It's fine,' said Jael, 'but try not to drag us into anything else, ok?'

Ryan nodded.

'You realise that when you fly off the handle like that you're only doing what the colonel wants?' pointed out Kev. 'That's the reaction he's after. And he'll keep messing with you until you stop fighting him. You're his new whipping boy.'

'I guess,' admitted Ryan. 'Sorry.'

He wasn't sure what else to say. But there was no way he would back down and let the colonel bully him into submission.

'Another thing,' teased Kev. 'Will you please stop apologising?'

'Yeah,' agreed Lee. 'It's annoying.'

Ryan almost made the mistake of saying 'sorry' again, but stopped himself. 'Ok,' he said instead. 'I'll try.'

12. RULES

After they had all changed out of the boiler suits, the lads gave Ryan a tour.

'You get to spend a bit of time relaxing in the evening,' said Lee. 'But don't forget to do any homework. They don't go easy on you here.'

'I've worked that much out,' replied Ryan.

'And you're not allowed out of the school building after dinner,' added Jael, 'unless you're with a teacher.'

'How would they know?' asked Ryan.

'Security is tight here,' said Kev. 'Soldiers patrol the grounds with guard dogs. There are alarms and cameras and stuff.'

'So don't go getting any smart ideas.' Jael gave him a dark look.

'And you don't think that's weird? For a school to have guards?' demanded Ryan.

'Like I said before, Ryan,' Lee reminded him, as if he was being slow, 'this isn't a normal school. The Project has enemies. It needs protecting.'

'But why?'

'Some of the stuff we work on here is top-secret,' Jael explained. 'Even the resources we have access to are dangerous or classified. The chemicals in our science lab, for instance.'

'And then there's the Outlier,' added Lee.

'The Outlier?'

'Devonmoor's number one enemy. Rumour has it he's the most intelligent student the academy ever had. But he turned rogue and wants payback.'

'For what?'

'Dunno,' admitted Lee. 'The teachers don't talk about it much. He didn't enjoy his time here, that's for sure. Given a chance, he'd take this place down.'

They were in the older part of the building, walking down a corridor. As they reached the end, they came to some large doors with brass handles. A golden plaque read: 'Library: Silence is to be observed at all times.'

'We can't speak in here,' said Lee. 'We'll walk you through so you can see what it's like. It's a good place to do homework.'

Lee pushed at the right-hand door and walked in. Ryan followed close behind him, surprised to find himself in such an enormous room. On the left were individual desks arranged in perfect rows, each with its own study lamp. Several of them were occupied by Devonmoor students hard at work. To the right were rows and rows of bookshelves.

What struck Ryan most was the intimidating silence in the place. It was quite an achievement given the number of students present. He guessed that was down to a couple of prefects in their black berets, who appeared to be standing guard. One of them looked up at the four lads and narrowed his eyes as a warning: get on with your work or get out. Lee grabbed Ryan's shoulder and led him back to the corridor.

'Nice place,' commented Ryan. 'Let me guess: if you talk in there then you get into trouble?'

'You see,' Lee turned to Kev and Jael, smiling, 'now he's catching on!'

'Can I just ask something?' continued Ryan. 'Is there anything you can do at this school *without* getting into trouble?' He was being serious but Lee laughed, which made Ryan nervous.

They descended a concrete staircase. At the bottom, a small door led into a cramped underground space which smelled of damp. Clothes lines stretched from wall to wall, full of grey-and-maroon uniforms, white vests and blue-and-yellow sports kits.

'This is the laundry room,' said Lee.

'We have to do our own washing,' cut in Jael, 'so in our dorm we take it in turns. It keeps everything easier. We'll show you how to use the machines sometime.'

'Really?' Ryan didn't like the idea of having to wash his own clothes, let alone sort through stuff the other lads had worn. At home, the cleaner did it all.

'Yeah, you're gonna have to pull your weight.' Jael was firm. Ryan didn't want to get in an argument so he stayed silent.

'Jael's right,' said Kev, noting the look on his face.

As he looked at the washing lines, Ryan had an idea. 'Wait. What stops you from dumping your dirty laundry in the corner and taking the stuff that's already clean?'

'Basic morality,' answered Jael, giving Ryan a scathing look.

'Well, that and the cameras,' added Lee, pointing to a small black dome on the ceiling. 'Besides, most of your clothes have your name written in them. And you don't want to get caught stealing other people's stuff.'

'Why? What happens?' Ryan was trying to get a grip on what kinds of punishments they dished out at Devonmoor.

'It depends on what you did, and why,' said Kev. 'But the last kid who got his washing mixed up with another cadet's had to do his entire corridor's laundry for a month. Trust me, that's a *lot* of washing.'

'That reminds me,' said Lee, 'we need to get you your own uniform. We'd better go and see Dr Fleur.'

They headed back up the stairs and into the grand entrance hall. Lee stopped by one of the doors and looked nervously at Kev.

'Fine, I'll do it,' sighed Kev, as if reading his mind. He stepped forward and knocked.

'Enter.'

They walked in to a sparse and unnaturally tidy office. There wasn't a single sheet of paper in sight. Behind a desk sat Dr Fleur, tapping away at her computer. She stopped and stared at the cadets, like a black widow spider eyeing up her lunch.

'I trust you have interrupted me for something important?' she asked. Kev took a small step forward.

'Yes ma'am. Jacobs here is new. He needs a

uniform.'

'And that takes four of you does it? Is Jacobs unable to speak?'

'No ma'am. Would you like us to wait outside?' Kev offered.

'I think that would be wise.'

Kev, Lee and Jael made for the door so fast that they almost tripped each other up. Ryan stayed where he was, not liking the way Dr Fleur was looking at him. She stood up.

'Against the wall.'

'What?' Ryan was confused.

'Now that you're a cadet here, you call me ma'am.'

'Yes, ma'am.'

'Now, against the wall.'

Ryan took a few steps backwards, unsure what she meant.

'For a genius, you're pretty slow, you know that? Turn around and put your hands on the wall.'

He did as he was told, feeling like he was being punished but not knowing why. Dr Fleur held something against his back and then wrapped it around his waist. A tape measure. He stood still while she did the same thing to his arms and legs, occasionally asking Ryan to change position. She pulled out a clipboard and made notes as she worked.

'What shoe size are you?'

'Seven.'

'Seven, *ma'am*,' said Dr Fleur, pointedly.

'Seven, ma'am,' Ryan repeated, already sick of

being told off. He hadn't even been here for a day yet.

'We are finished here, cadet. Your uniform and sports kit will be delivered to your room later tonight. It will be your responsibility to keep it clean, and to ensure that you are presentable at all times.'

'Yes, ma'am.'

'You may leave.'

Ryan hurried out before she gave him any more orders.

'How was it?' asked Lee.

'Great,' said Ryan. 'It was like being strip-searched. She said she'd deliver the uniform to our room tonight.'

Kev laughed. 'That's Dr Fleur for you. Come on, let's finish this tour so we can get to the common room before lights out.'

The boys decided there was one other place Ryan needed to see: a large sports hall with basketball hoops at either end and a polished floor.

'This is where we have drill,' said Lee, his voice echoing off the hard walls. 'Every weekday morning we have to show up here and they inspect our uniform, give us notices, stuff like that.'

'Sounds fun,' said Ryan, glumly.

'It's not too bad,' said Lee, with his usual sunny optimism. 'Once you know what you're doing, it's pretty easy.'

'As long as you do as you're told,' muttered Jael.

'Have they shown you the basics: how to salute and stand to attention and stuff?' asked Kev.

'Yeah, I think so,' said Ryan, 'Dr Torren taught me

all that before I met with the Board.'

'Well don't screw it up,' said Kev. 'If you do then we all get into trouble.'

'I'll try not to,' replied Ryan. But as they climbed back up the stairs, Ryan remembered the colonel's words: *I sure feel sorry for you boys... God knows how much trouble he'll cause.*

There were too many rules here. It was way too strict. And much as he didn't want to admit it, the colonel was probably right.

13. DOWNTIME

Ryan cheered up when he saw the common room. The vast room extended over the dormitories below. It had started out as the loft of the accommodation block, but now the sloping ceilings, the skylights, and the long, narrow run of the room all added to its character.

Soft chairs and sofas were spread out between the beams, creating comfortable areas to sit and relax. Towards the back, two pool tables and a ping-pong table were surrounded by groups of cadets waiting to take a turn.

A few of the seating areas had large TVs, one of which had a games console attached. A radio station could be heard over the general noise.

'Wow,' said Ryan, amazed. 'This place is awesome.'

'Yeah, it is,' admitted Lee, 'and this is what we'd have missed out on if you hadn't done as the colonel asked!' He gave Ryan a playful shove, and Ryan smiled.

'Can we come in here whenever we want?'

'Evenings and weekends,' said Kev, 'but they ban everyone from using it if standards have dropped.'

'Or exclude people from particular dormitories,'

added Jael. 'It's a pretty effective way to keep people in line.'

Ryan could understand that. Life at Devonmoor wouldn't be too bad with a state-of-the-art computing lab and a fun room like this to relax in.

A loud voice cut through his thoughts: 'Everyone stand back! Jacobs is here! He might puke!'

A few people laughed and Ryan turned to see Ayana, the girl who had been unfortunate enough to be sat next to him in the helicopter.

'How you settling in?' she asked.

'Well it looks like I'm staying,' he replied, 'but I'll try not to throw up on you too often, I promise.'

She nodded. 'Well, I guess it wasn't your fault.'

Ryan was relieved that she wasn't holding a grudge.

'Hey, Jael,' shouted one lad, sitting next to a chess board. 'Want to play?'

'Sure,' said Jael, heading over, 'if you want to lose.'

'Jael's incredible at chess,' Lee explained to Ryan. 'He ranks pretty high in the world. That's what got him here.'

'Chess?' asked Ryan. 'Why would the academy want a good chess player?'

'His specialism isn't just chess,' cut in Ayana. 'Jael thinks in patterns. He has a knack for identifying strong correlations and dismissing irrelevant data. It makes him great at those kinds of games.'

That figured.

'So what's your specialism?' Ryan asked, turning

to Kev. 'Do you have one?'

'Yeah,' said Kev, 'everyone does. Mine is strategy, leadership and negotiation: that sort of stuff.'

'Kev was captain of the under-12's England rugby squad,' Lee added, 'but he was also voted on to the Junior Cabinet.'

'The Junior Cabinet?' Ryan had never heard of it.

'It's a politics thing, to get kids involved. But you have to be pretty good to get on it. No-one had ever made it at age eleven before. The youngest member until then had been fourteen.'

'And you learn stuff really quick?' Ryan asked Lee.

'That's one way to put it,' cut in Ayana. 'He's lucky enough to have a photographic memory.'

'How about you?' Ryan asked her. 'What's your skill?'

'Languages. And cultures. There are subtle differences in the way people in different countries think. They bring new perspectives to problem-solving.'

He looked around. Everyone seemed so normal. It was hard to imagine that they were the cleverest kids in the country. 'Who's Jael playing chess with?' he asked.

The boy was their age. He was the fattest person there, and had brown, curly hair and small round glasses.

'That's Kelvin Sparks,' answered Lee. 'He's a laugh. Complete genius with building stuff. His specialism is engineering.'

'So how did they find him?' asked Ryan, curious.

'Sparks got into making robots when he was, like, aged six. There are these clubs where you get to battle your robots against each other and his kept winning.'

'And the kid next to him?' asked Ryan.

'Ranjit Jeet? He's Dr Torren's star pupil. He can tell what you're thinking, when you're lying and stuff. Never play poker with him.'

'Thanks for the heads up.'

As he continued to scan the room, Ryan noticed the tall girl who had escorted him from the computer lab. She was sitting with a few of her friends, laughing. He stared at her for too long because Kev picked up on it.

'Not a chance,' he said, placing his hand on Ryan's shoulder. 'Way out of your league, mate.'

'Who is she?' he asked.

'Sarah Devonmoor. Lady Devonmoor's granddaughter no less.'

'So what's her specialism?'

'Breaking lads' hearts,' joked Kev, 'and she's good at it. Come on, let's play pool.'

***

Later that evening, all four boys were back in their room. Ryan was sorting through the pile of neatly folded clothes that had been left on his bed. Along with the grey jackets and trousers, there were several identical pairs of black boxers and five pairs of long grey socks. Next to them sat loads of sports kit: blue rugby shirts with thin yellow stripes, blue running vests, white shorts and plain yellow football socks. There was even a canvas bag with the 'Devonmoor Academy' logo embroidered on it, a golden hawk soaring through the air.

Next to Ryan's bed were some black shiny boots in a size seven and a pair of white trainers. It was a lot of stuff and he should have been pleased, but then he remembered that this was all he had—the sum total of his possessions at Devonmoor.

Lee helped him to stash it in the wardrobe while the others got ready for lights out.

'I don't get it. Why do I need so many rugby kits?' asked Ryan, picking up a shirt. It looked like the kind of thing schoolkids would have worn fifty years ago.

'We wear them for all sports,' explained Lee, 'and we do a lot of physical training here.'

'You get pretty muddy,' added Jael. 'You need spare kit for when your stuff is in the wash.'

Ryan thought of his grimy football kit at home. 'What happens if you wear dirty kit?'

'Don't ask.' Kev looked at him with a serious expression.

'Just curious.'

Ryan finished stuffing the clothes in a drawer, as the other lads stripped off their trousers and jackets and crashed into bed in their boxers. Ryan didn't even bother to take his socks off.

'You need to get up and dressed quickly in the morning,' said Lee. 'You get five minutes from the wake up call to get to drill.'

'Ok,' said Ryan. 'I'll follow you guys.'

Jael was sitting on his bed rubbing his boots with a buffing device. He seemed to be making a pretty thorough job of it. He saw Ryan watching him.

'Hey, you should do yours as well,' he said, throwing him the polish.

Ryan lifted the boots. 'Nah, it's alright, they're new.'

Jael glanced towards Kev—a meaningful look.

'Err, no, you need to sort them out, mate,' urged Jael. 'Even new boots need to be polished. It won't take long.'

Ryan was tired of being told what to do. 'I'm not wasting my time cleaning a brand-new pair of boots.'

Jael sighed, unhappy but defeated.

'I'll do it,' offered Lee, picking up the polish.

'You don't have to,' said Ryan, now feeling guilty. 'It's not a big deal.'

'Not to you perhaps,' replied Jael, lying back on his bed, 'but you'll get the whole dormitory into trouble. You heard the colonel. He's going to be on your case, which means every time you screw up we all get punished.'

Lee was already hard at work on the boots.

'You worry too much,' said Ryan.

'Mate, you have no idea how harsh the colonel is,' warned Kev. 'He doesn't even need a reason. He likes to see people suffer.'

'Whatever.'

The dorm room settled into an uneasy silence.

A few minutes later there was the sound of the

doors locking and the lights went out.

It was Ryan's second night at Devonmoor.

And this time he had no hope of escape.

14. DRILL

That siren was seriously annoying.

Ryan was in a deep sleep when it cut right through his dreams, shocking him awake. He rubbed his eyes but didn't have enough energy to get up. The lack of sleep from the previous night had caught up with him.

'Ryan!' said Lee, shaking him. 'Come on! Get up! We don't have much time.'

Ryan knew he should. He knew the others were depending on him. He had been determined to make an effort, to try to follow the rules. But it was *so early*.

Ryan was not a morning person. He rolled over and closed his eyes. 'I don't feel great,' he mumbled into the pillow. 'You guys go without me.'

'No, mate, we only have a couple of minutes to get to drill,' explained Lee.

Ryan didn't respond.

'You have to get up!' shouted Jael, frustrated at Ryan's lack of movement. He was getting on Ryan's nerves.

'I don't *have* to do anything,' Ryan countered, opening his eyes. 'Leave me alone. I'll be fine.'

'What do we do?' Jael looking at the other lads, clearly worried.

'We can't force him to get up,' reasoned Kev, 'and

we're running late ourselves. We'll explain it to the drill sergeant and hope for the best.'

'This is bad. This is really bad. Why did we get stuck with him?'

Ryan turned and faced the wall, ignoring the lads as they finished dressing and left the room. Jael slammed the door.

Why is everyone on my case? thought Ryan. He couldn't help it if he needed more sleep than they did. Why was drill so important, anyway?

Now the other boys had left, everything was peaceful and Ryan dozed off.

***

Confusion.

Pain.

Water, so much water.

It happened so fast that Ryan didn't know what was going on. He spluttered for breath. Whichever way he moved, the water seemed to follow.

He swore, trying to get out from the powerful jet stream, rolling off the bottom bunk and hitting the tiles hard, taking the soaking-wet sheets with him.

It stopped. Ryan looked up.

James Sarrell stood over him, smirking as Ryan cowered on the floor. He was holding a fire extinguisher, the nozzle pointing straight at Ryan.

'Did you enjoy your lie in?' he asked, and then pressed the trigger again, releasing another barrage of water.

'Stop,' screamed Ryan, curling into a ball to shelter himself from the worst of the blast. 'STOP!'

Sarrell held on for a few more seconds. Ryan couldn't have been any wetter if he'd climbed out of a river. The vest, boxers and socks he was wearing clung to his body, freezing cold and dripping wet. He shivered as he half-lay, half-knelt in a huge puddle on the tiles. His bed was saturated.

'Are you INSANE?' yelled Ryan. 'Look what you've done!'

'You have five minutes to get into your uniform and down to the drill hall,' replied Sarrell.

'You can't be serious!' shouted Ryan. 'You can't do this!'

'Watch me,' spat Sarrell, pulling the trigger again. Ryan tried in vain to protect himself.

'Ok, ok,' Ryan coughed and spluttered on the floor. 'I'll do it. Just stop with the fire extinguisher.'

Sarrell laughed. He let off an extra burst of water before leaving the room.

Ryan wasn't only wet. His body hurt. He was sure that you should never use those things on people at close range.

Climbing to his feet, he changed into his uniform, trying not to drag the dry clothes through the standing water. Then he stormed down the corridor.

They can't do that! he fumed to himself. *It's not legal!*

The rage had built to such a crescendo by the time he reached the double doors that he threw them open, banging them hard against the wall as he strode into the gym.

The other cadets all stood in lines, spaced evenly apart. At the front was the drill sergeant: a young clean-shaven man in a military uniform.

'What the hell do you think you're doing, cadet?' the man yelled at him.

'ME?' roared Ryan, walking right up to the sergeant's face. 'What the hell do you think YOU'RE doing? You can't use fire extinguishers on students! I'm reporting you. I'm reporting this school!'

The sergeant didn't look concerned. 'I don't know what you're talking about, cadet.'

'Sarrell! That's what I'm talking about! He let loose on me with a fire extinguisher! Just cause I'm late for your stupid drill.' Ryan's eyes blazed, daring the man to contradict him.

'If another cadet has been bullying you then you might have grounds for a complaint,' remarked the man, coolly, 'but is there any reason why you feel Cadet Sarrell should follow the rules while you get away with breaking them?'

'No,' spluttered Ryan, unsure of himself for the first time in the dispute. 'No, but I...' He trailed off, lost for words. He'd been so sure, so confident that he was in the right. But now he was standing in front of the entire school and he realised he was a hypocrite. It wasn't a great time to have that kind of insight.

'Jacobs, they warned me that you had an attitude problem. As things stand, your whole dormitory will report for drill an hour early tomorrow,' warned the sergeant. 'I suggest you take your place in line, unless you'd like to make things worse for them? Is that what you want?'

Ryan was tired, and he knew it; he wasn't thinking clearly.

'No, sir.'

He hung his head and shuffled over to the end of the line, knowing that he'd once again dragged his new friends into trouble. At this rate, they wouldn't stay friends for long.

Get a grip, Ryan.

Either he was going to learn to play by the academy's rules or he was going to end up humiliated and alone.

15. STRATEGY

'What part of *you have to get up* do you not understand!' Jael fumed as they left the sports hall. Lee and Kev looked angry and disappointed.

'Seriously, Ryan,' agreed Lee. 'That was not cool.'

'And don't you dare say you're sorry again,' Jael continued. 'I don't care if you're sorry. We still lose an hour of sleep tomorrow thanks to you!'

Ryan didn't know how to respond. If he wasn't allowed to apologise then he wasn't sure what they wanted.

'I'll try to do better,' he offered, weakly.

'Whatever.' Jael stormed off.

'What is with you?' demanded Kev. 'How stupid can you be? Do you enjoy getting into trouble?'

Jael whining at him seemed par for the course—he found the kid irritating—but he had serious respect for Kev so this last comment cut deep.

'It's taking me a while to settle in,' he mumbled. 'What can I say?'

'I don't think saying anything is going to help,' Kev replied. 'In fact, the less you say the better. I can't even look at you right now.'

'Ok, ok, ' Ryan was getting defensive. 'I get the message.'

Lee shuffled his feet. 'We should get to breakfast.'

They headed to the canteen. Ryan was glad that the verbal beating was over but he got the distinct impression that the others weren't going to let this drop. His mood didn't improve when he scored two out of five on the canteen test which only got him toast and butter. He sat at the same table as Kev and Lee.

Kelvin Sparks sat next to Ryan, putting down a plate full of sausages, eggs and bacon. 'Morning,' he said, cheerfully, failing to recognise the tension between the lads.

Kev nodded to him, his mouth full.

'Hi Sparks,' replied Lee, looking tired.

'We've not met yet,' the boy said to Ryan. 'I'm Kelvin, but everyone calls me Sparks.'

'I'm Ryan, Ryan Jacobs.'

'I've never seen anyone have a go at Sergeant Wright like that in drill!' Sparks sounded both amused and impressed. 'You have some nerve!'

'Don't encourage him,' warned Kev.

'Well, I'm not saying it was a clever thing to do,' Sparks grinned, 'but come on, it was entertaining!'

Ryan smiled a little, but with Lee and Kev sitting there he didn't want to appear as if he wasn't sorry for the whole incident. He decided it might be a good idea to change the subject. 'I hear you're pretty good at building stuff?' he asked.

'Yeah, robots mostly,' Kelvin said with his mouth full of bacon, 'but also vehicles and other stuff. What do you do?'

'Computers,' answered Ryan. 'I'm a hacker.'

'That's so cool!' Sparks was enthusiastic and Ryan couldn't help liking him. 'So how are you finding Devonmoor?'

'It's good,' admitted Ryan, 'mostly.'

Lee glanced in Ryan's direction with an I-told-you-so kind of expression.

'I saw what happened in the canteen yesterday,' continued Sparks. 'I had hassle when I arrived here too. I'm not your usual military cadet!'

'Did you get badly bullied?'

'A little,' shrugged Sparks. 'But a lot was just friendly banter.'

'Well, apart from the Hayes incident,' laughed Kev. 'No-one dared pick on him after that!'

'The Hayes incident?' asked Ryan.

'Cadet Hayes. He was laying into Sparks,' explained Lee. 'Every other day he'd punch him in the canteen and make his life a misery. Then one day Sparks wired up a device under his uniform that gave Hayes a several-thousand-volt electric shock when he punched it.'

'Did it work?' Ryan asked.

'Oh yeah,' said Kev, grinning, 'for sure. Hayes was shaking on the floor for over ten minutes. The shock made him cack his pants. He never lived it down!'

'I might have been a little over-generous with the voltage,' acknowledged Sparks, winking at Ryan. 'He never bothered me again.'

'Maybe I need something like that for Sarrell?' Ryan glanced over to where the mean-looking cadet sat with a bunch of older students.

'Well,' replied Sparks, mopping up his fried egg with the last piece of his bread, 'I wouldn't recommend it. I had detention for a fortnight, but it was *so* worth it.'

***

As they left the canteen, Lee led Ryan to a classroom. Before going in, he pulled him aside.

'Our first lesson today is strategy, and Colonel Keller teaches us,' he warned Ryan. 'He'll do his best to wind you up. You've got to keep control of yourself and not get us in any more trouble, ok?'

'Ok,' nodded Ryan. He had to prove to Lee and the others that he could stop acting out.

Lee looked Ryan's uniform up and down. He grabbed the zipper on Ryan's jacket and pulled it right up to the neck. 'Are you ready?' he asked Ryan.

'As ready as I'll ever be.' He followed Lee in.

The first thing he noticed was that the room was empty—there were no chairs or desks at all. Daylight streamed in through windows along the back, which overlooked the muddy sports fields. The walls were khaki green. At the front was a small stage area. Colonel Keller stood on it, watching the cadets file in. Behind him was an old-fashioned blackboard.

As each cadet entered the room, they turned to face the front and snapped to attention. Ryan noticed that there were small red lines marked on the floor which showed where you were meant to stand. He took his place at one and copied the others.

The colonel was watching him, but Ryan didn't make eye contact. As the last cadet entered, Ryan could sense the tension in the room.

'At ease, cadets,' said the colonel.

They all relaxed their stance, but not too much.

'Today we will be exploring Game Theory,' he began. 'It's a branch of mathematics that plays an important role in military strategy. With Game Theory you can predict what a person is going to do, what they will choose from the options available. If you know how they will act, you can prepare for it. That's how you beat them.'

The colonel turned to the blackboard and, gripping the chalk, he wrote out a word in capital letters: 'ULTIMATUM'.

'Our first game is Ultimatum,' he said, turning back to the cadets. 'It's the simplest of the games, and it involves two players. Here's how it works.' The colonel walked up and down the small stage. 'Let's imagine that there are ten cookies. Player One can choose how many cookies they want to keep, and how many they will give to Player Two. Player Two can choose to either accept or reject the offer that Player One makes. If they reject it, then neither of the players get any cookies at all. Player Two has been given an ultimatum. It may not be a fair one, but his only option is to accept or reject it. Do you understand the rules of the game?'

'Yes, sir,' responded the cadets in unison. Ryan understood, but it didn't sound like much of a fun game.

'Do you have any thoughts?' asked the colonel. 'What do you think is likely to happen when the game is played for real?'

A few hands went up, much to Ryan's surprise. He hadn't expected anyone to risk getting the answer wrong. The colonel pointed to a girl on Ryan's left.

'Cadet Lynch?'

'If Player One splits the cookies evenly, then Player Two would accept. Otherwise they would probably reject the offer.'

'But then they would get no cookies at all,' countered the colonel, 'and even a couple of cookies would be better than none, wouldn't they?'

Cadet Lynch looked confused.

'Adams?' The colonel nodded to a boy at the front who looked keen.

'Sir, if they were being rational, Player Two would agree to any offer that involved them getting at least one cookie. That means that Player One could keep nine and offer Player Two one, and they would still accept it.'

'But that hardly seems fair now, does it?' asked the colonel.

'War isn't fair, sir,' responded the cadet. 'Player Two is not in a position to bargain. They have to take the best deal they can, and anything is better than nothing.'

'Yes!' It was weird seeing Colonel Keller get enthusiastic. 'Precisely! Well done, Adams. That is exactly how this game works. In terms of war, of course, we're not going to be giving our enemy cookies. However, we can use the same principles to ensure a lose-lose outcome for our opponents.' The colonel drew himself up to his full height. 'For those of you who still have your doubts, I think a demonstration may be in order. Let's have two volunteers. Jeet and Jacobs, I think. Come and stand up here.'

Ryan swallowed hard and tried to stay calm as he stepped up on to the platform, taking his place next to Ranjit Jeet.

'Cadet Jeet,' stated the colonel. 'You will be Player One. Jacobs, you are Player Two. The prize is ten hours of cleaning duty. Jeet, you can make an offer to Jacobs of how many of those hours you will do, and how many he will do. Jacobs, you can either take or reject the offer. If you reject it, then both of you will work for a full ten hours. Do you understand?'

'Yes, sir,' they both responded, less than enthusiastic.

'And remember,' added the colonel, 'fairness is not a consideration in this game. You play for the optimum outcome for yourself.'

Great, thought Ryan. *That's just great.*

He'd worked out by now what was coming.

'In which case,' Ranjit said, 'the obvious thing would be for me to offer Jacobs nine hours, while I only do one?'

'That would be the optimum solution,' agreed the colonel. 'Is that your offer?'

'Yes, sir.' Ranjit looked apologetically at Ryan.

'So, Jacobs now has two options: to work for ten hours, or to only do nine. Well, what's it to be?'

Ryan wanted to choose ten, to spite the colonel and to prove that you don't have to allow yourself to be bullied. But he figured that would be harsh on Ranjit who would then also have to do ten hours. It wasn't the other boy's fault; the colonel had forced him to make the harshest offer. Ryan could hardly hold that against him. Besides, Ryan was trying to make friends at Devonmoor, not lose them.

'Nine, sir,' muttered Ryan.

'Excellent,' said the colonel. 'And that is how this game works. What's the trick to winning, do you think?'

There was a brief pause before Cadet Lynch's hand shot up.

'To make sure you're Player One?' she suggested.

'Exactly. Make sure you're the one calling the shots. They have to learn that you're in charge.' The colonel turned to Ryan and Ranjit. 'Both of you report to me at four o'clock to begin your cleaning. Any complaints, Jacobs?'

Ryan summoned up all the self-resolve he could muster. 'No sir,' he lied.

'It seems you're learning. Stand back in line.'

Ryan did as he was told, trying to keep his temper in check. He'd just got nine hours of cleaning for no reason at all. He wanted to object, but he knew the colonel would love him to make a scene. It wasn't worth it, however unfair it was. The other lads were right: the more he reacted, the more the colonel would make his life miserable. For now, he needed to take it without complaining.

And so, Ryan stood in line for the remainder of the strategy lesson, feeling a certain sense of achievement. Maybe he could get control of his temper and learn to follow the rules after all.

And nothing would annoy the colonel more than that.

16. TUNNEL

An hour later, Ryan had almost forgotten about the colonel's game. He was in the boys' changing room, pulling on dull-yellow football socks. For some stupid reason, you only got to wear long socks at Devonmoor. It was starting to bug him.

'Hey, Jacobs, are you fast?'

Ryan turned to see Jason Humphreys, a lad he'd met in the common room. 'Fairly. Why?'

'Today is cross-country. We split into teams and do a long run followed by a circuit of the assault course.'

'Sounds good.'

A whistle sounded outside and everyone hurried on to the sports field. It was a grey October day, chilly but not freezing. The cadets lined up along the edge of a football pitch, their feet touching the line. Sergeant Wright, the drill instructor, stood at the front.

'Right, everyone, form yourselves into teams of three,' he ordered. There was a moment of chaos.

Ryan ended up with Jason and Lee. He was grateful that they were happy to include him, saving him any awkwardness.

'Today you'll be doing a three-mile run followed by the assault course. The team that comes first will get a first class lunch. Whichever team comes last will repeat the exercise on Saturday morning. Is that clear?'

'Yes, sir,' responded the cadets.

'I said IS THAT CLEAR?' Sergeant Wright yelled.

'YES, SIR!' the cadets shouted back.

'You know the route. Get ready.'

'Follow us,' Jason whispered, and Ryan nodded.

The teacher blew hard on the whistle and everyone shot across the field, working their way towards the woods. Ryan stuck close to Jason and Lee, surprised at how fast everyone was. Surely they weren't planning to keep up that pace for three miles?

He forced himself to keep going. The next few minutes were hell, but his body eased into a rhythm. A few teams overtook them as they ran down the path between the trees.

'Come on, Ryan!' said Jason, glancing back, 'I think Sparks is quicker than you!'

Ryan was too tired to comment, but his cheeks burned. The trail was muddy and the cheap trainers weren't doing much to keep the water out. It wasn't long before his legs were splattered with mud and both of his feet were soaked.

He was used to being one of the faster kids at his old school—his football training kept him fit—but here at Devonmoor everyone exercised hard, and it showed. Despite his best efforts he was slowing the team down. Most of the others had passed by the time they reached the assault course, but only just. It wasn't a lost cause; they could still do this.

The first obstacle seemed easy enough: crossing a muddy ditch using horizontal logs. Ryan dashed across, as quick as Jason and Lee. He noticed an older cadet in a black beret watching, making sure no-one cheated.

Next was a vertical wall. His teammates seemed to know what they were doing. Jason gave Lee a leg-up and then asked Ryan to do the same for him.

'Take a running jump,' Jason said to Ryan, 'and then grab my hand and I'll pull you up.'

Ryan took a few steps back and ran at the wall, but his wet trainers slipped on the logs. He climbed to his feet, rubbing his knee.

'Try again,' urged Jason, 'but don't climb with your feet. Focus on getting your arms on top!'

Ryan followed his advice, jumping as high as he could. This time, Jason was able to grab hold of him, helping pull his body over. They dropped down the other side, panting.

'We're still at the back!' pointed out Lee, worried.

'Not for long!' Jason dashed forwards.

A set of tyres hung over the ditch. The three lads clambered over them, clinging to the ropes.

'What now?' Ryan asked.

'The tunnel,' shouted Lee, 'come on!'

He pointed to a circular opening in the ground: the end of a large pipe. Ryan crouched down and looked in. He could see daylight several metres away. He broke into a cold sweat.

'I-I-I can't do that!' he stuttered, his face white.

'What?' replied Jason, already on his stomach at

the entrance. 'Why not? It's easy.'

'I don't like small spaces,' explained Ryan.

'Mate, it's alright,' said Lee. 'It doesn't take long, and it's completely safe. I've done it loads of times.'

Jason was already pulling himself in.

'You go next,' Lee encouraged Ryan. 'I'll be right behind you.'

Ryan was torn. He took another look. Maybe it would be ok, he reasoned. He could at least see the end. His team were depending on him.

'Go on, Ryan,' urged Lee, gently pushing him. 'You need to hurry. The quicker you do it, the quicker you'll be out the other side.'

Ryan took a deep breath and pulled his body in. Little by little he edged forward, focusing on the circle of light at the other end. He swallowed as the darkness closed around him.

It was a mistake. The pipe got smaller and smaller the further he went. As he tried to pick up pace his back scraped the top. He panicked and tried to thrash his arms, banging his elbow. He couldn't move his legs.

Ryan wanted to scream, but it felt like something was jammed in his throat. It made him cough and retch.

And then it all started flooding back.

All of it.

Just like he was there.

***

It was pitch black. He lay next to the cold ground. His face was a mess—all blood and broken glass— and he could feel sharp splinters in his cheek and forehead.

But that wasn't the worst of it.

His leg screamed at him. It was trapped in a vice that was getting tighter and tighter, crushing it with intense pressure. Any moment now, his bone would splinter.

Ryan called out in the darkness, but no-one seemed to hear. He was boxed in—he couldn't even move his arms. He shouted again.

A sharp piece of metal protruded from his shoulder. Whenever he shifted his weight, pain seared through his upper back. He tried to keep still, tensing his stomach, but his torso moved every time he breathed. Hot, sticky blood covered everything.

He'd been told that people passed out when the pain got too bad and he shut his eyes and tried to make it happen, but his heart was beating a thousand times a minute. There was no chance of drifting into unconsciousness, no hope of relief. He could feel it all.

And worse, he could smell burning. He knew that all it took was for the fire to reach the fuel tank and there would be an explosion. Or maybe he would burn alive as he lay here. Either way, he would die.

He shouted again, and then screamed, but it made no difference. The heat rose. He could see the flames now, flickering a short distance in front of him.

'Help!' he shouted. 'HELP!'

The smoke got in his lungs and he coughed, his head scraping on the broken glass. He spluttered and gasped for clean air but knew he only had seconds.

In that moment Ryan knew it was over.

He was going to die.

And it was going to hurt.

It was really going to hurt.

***

'Ryan, RYAN!' shouted Lee.

Ryan was banging his fists against the sides of the pipe and tears were streaming down his face. He *had* to get out!

A hand grabbed his leg and Lee dragged him out by his ankle, back into the daylight.

'What the hell?' asked Lee, looking concerned. 'What's wrong with you?'

Ryan moaned as he lay in the mud. His heart was beating fast—too fast. Lee was leaning over him, but he seemed a long way off, his blond hair shining like a halo.

'I-I-I...' stuttered Ryan.

'Dammit Ryan, have you wet yourself?' Lee sounded more distant now; concerned rather than angry.

Ryan didn't answer.

Nothing mattered anymore. Not even that.

He closed his eyes, his brain shut down, and the world went black.

17. RECOVERY

When he regained consciousness, he was lying on something soft. People were speaking nearby. Ryan didn't open his eyes. He wasn't ready to face the world.

He had vague memories of being carried back to the school, being stripped of his clothes and held under a warm shower. Then they brought him here: the medical room. A room with an overpowering smell of disinfectant. He'd wanted to object. He hated places like this. He'd spent too much of his life in them. But he didn't say anything.

He pretended to be asleep as he listened to the conversation next to him. It wasn't hard to work out who it was: the smooth, hypnotic voice of Dr Torren and the gentle words of Lady Devonmoor.

'... whenever he is in those conditions the memories flood back,' the doctor was saying. 'He hasn't got over the car accident. I can't say I blame him. It says in his file that Jacobs was stuck in that wreck for over half an hour. They had to cut him out. They barely got there in time, before he was burned alive. He was in hospital for over two months after the event.'

'Poor boy,' said the head-teacher. 'Can you cure

him?'

'We can try,' Dr Torren reassured her, 'though patients vary in their response to treatment. Not all treatment is successful. And it takes time.'

'Well we must do what we can. When can the treatment begin? When he's conscious?'

'Oh, he's conscious now,' stated Dr Torren. 'He just hasn't realised he's naked yet.'

Naked?

Ryan's eyes shot open, and he lifted his head. He wasn't naked—he was wearing a pair of boxers—but as he looked up, he saw Dr Torren smiling.

'Hello, Jacobs,' he said. 'I thought that might get a response.'

'How long have I been here?' asked Ryan, feeling stupid for falling for the doctor's trick.

'About an hour, dear.' Lady Devonmoor stepped towards him and ran her hand through his dark hair. 'How are you feeling?'

'I'm fine.' He felt awkward lying in his underwear with Lady Devonmoor stroking him like a cute pet. 'Where are my clothes?' he asked, pointedly. They both ignored the question.

'Jacobs,' said Dr Torren, looking at him with those piercing blue eyes, 'has that kind of thing ever happened to you before?'

'Yeah... no... I don't want to talk about it,' stuttered Ryan, looking away. 'I just want to get dressed and get out of here.'

'Fair enough. Why don't we send you back to Sergeant Wright so you can complete the assault course?'

The look of fear on Ryan's face betrayed him.

'It happens every time you're in a confined space, doesn't it?' Dr Torren enquired.

Ryan's eyes filled with tears. 'Only in tiny spaces,' he said, his voice wavering, 'if I can't move my arms and legs and I feel trapped. I never used to be claustrophobic, but after the accident...'

'So you're ok in cars, and lifts and things like that?'

Ryan nodded. 'You'd think I'd be nervous in cars. I was the first few times, but then it was ok.'

'Do your parents know?'

Ryan shook his head. 'I managed to hide it.'

'I don't think you're just claustrophobic, Jacobs,' said Dr Torren. 'I think you have Post-Traumatic Stress Disorder. We can try to help you with it, but you *will* have to talk.'

Ryan wiped the tears from his eyes with the back of his hand and looked at the doctor, who wasn't going to take no for an answer. Ryan let his head sink back into the pillow. 'Fine, but not right now, ok? I want my clothes!'

'Ok,' said Dr Torren, satisfied. 'We'll get them sent in.'

'It's good to see you're ok, dear,' said Lady Devonmoor, squeezing his hand. 'I hope you feel better soon.' She followed the doctor out, leaving Ryan alone.

He groaned as he remembered that he'd wet himself in the tunnel. He'd never live that down. Had he screamed? Had he lashed out at anyone? He'd probably said something rude, or embarrassing, or stupid. Maybe all three.

Way to go, Ryan. Way to make everyone think you're a freak.

Now everyone would start asking questions.

And that would only make things worse.

***

They let him out of the medical room at lunchtime, and Ryan headed to the canteen. He filed into the queue for food behind Ranjit who turned and smiled.

'Hey,' he said. 'Thanks so much for earlier. It sucked what the colonel did. I wanted to go halves with you, but I think he'd have punished us both.'

Ryan had almost forgotten the strategy lesson. Now it all came back to him. 'Yeah, I think so too. I'm going to have a tough time until he gets bored with punishing me.'

'He really doesn't like you, does he?' asked Ranjit.

'No,' admitted Ryan. 'I was caught hacking, so he figures I'm a criminal and don't belong here. He thinks I'll wreck the Project or something.'

'That figures,' Ranjit said. 'Anyway, I owe you one.'

The lads reached the computer terminals for the canteen test. Ryan noticed that at least two of the five questions related to stuff they'd covered in yesterday's lessons. He got both of them right, and answered another by pure fluke, which earned him a plate of sausage and mash. He made his way over to his room-mates, who were all sitting at their usual table with Jason, Sparks and Ayana.

'Ryan!' exclaimed Lee, concerned. 'Are you ok?'

'Yeah, I'm fine. Sorry about that.'

'It was our fault,' admitted Lee. 'We shouldn't have made you go into the tunnel.'

'Mate, you went skitz in there,' added Jason. 'You freaked out.'

'I'm assuming we lost the race?' asked Ryan.

'Yeah, but thanks to you Sergeant Wright let us off doing the run this Saturday.'

'Awesome.'

'Is it true that the colonel gave you nine hours of cleaning duty?' asked Ayana, horrified at the prospect.

'Yeah, I didn't do anything wrong either.'

'For once,' muttered Jael, but as Ryan caught his eye, he saw Jael was smiling.

'Were you impressed?' he asked him. 'That I didn't have a go at the colonel or anything?'

Jael shrugged, taking a spoonful of mash. 'I'll be impressed if you survive all nine hours without getting into worse trouble.'

'Yeah,' agreed Kev, who was sitting opposite. 'Let's face it, Ryan, you're doomed. The chances of that are close to zero. He's gonna wind you right up.'

'It'll be ok,' said Ryan. 'I'll manage it. I think I'm getting the hang of it.'

Kev caught Jael's eye, unconvinced. 'Well,' he nodded. 'That's a better attitude at least. Good luck.'

***

As the last lesson ended, Ryan made his way to the colonel's classroom, psyching himself up for the ordeal ahead.

He knocked on the door and waited.

'Come in.'

Ranjit was already there, standing to attention. Ryan marched to the spot next to him and saluted. The colonel looked at him with narrowed eyes, as if daring him to say something. He stayed silent.

Eventually, the colonel spoke. 'Follow me.'

He marched them to the block of changing rooms at the far end of the sports field. By now they were even more filthy than before, the tiled walls and floor streaked with mud from the assault course.

The colonel opened a cupboard, revealing basic equipment: brushes, a mop and various other cleaning products. He handed the mop to Ranjit.

'Cadet Jeet, the bucket needs to be filled with water from the outside tap. Use two capfuls of the floor cleaning liquid with it. You'll need to mop the floor at least twice; once to get the worst of this up and the second time to make sure it's clean. All the towels and lost property need to be taken to the laundry where you will wash them. You clean both this changing room and the one next door. Any questions?'

'No sir.' responded Ranjit, but Ryan could guess what he was thinking: *How the hell am I meant to do all of that in an hour?*

'Good. Begin.'

Ranjit grabbed the mop and got to work.

'Now, Jacobs,' said the colonel. 'I have a special job for you.' He picked up some heavy-duty rubber gloves, a cleaning spray and a small wiry brush. He led Ryan to the showers. 'You see the dirt and limescale that's built up between the tiles?'

'Yes, sir,' responded Ryan, a sinking feeling in his stomach.

'That's what you're going to be cleaning for the next few days. You will come to this changing room, collect the materials from the cupboard and start scrubbing. I want you here between four and six today and tomorrow, and then again on Saturday from eight in the morning. At lunchtime I will come and inspect your work and I expect to see these showers looking like new. Anything you want to say?'

'No, sir,' said Ryan.

'Are you sure you don't want to tell me how it isn't fair, or how you'd rather not do it? Or shout abuse at me?'

'No, sir.' Ryan kept his face neutral.

'I'm almost disappointed, Jacobs. Don't tell me I've broken your spirit that easily?'

Ryan wasn't sure if that was a proper question or not. He stayed silent.

'Well,' continued the colonel, after a brief pause, 'let's see if your new attitude holds up. I will check on you, and if you're not working hard, then *bad* things happen. Do I make myself clear?'

'Yes, sir,' replied Ryan.

'Good. Get to work.'

Ryan pulled on the gloves and started scrubbing. At the top of the wall there was barely any scum but the further he worked his way down, the worse it got. He'd never cleaned a bathroom, and it was hard work. The colonel paced back and forth, giving orders.

'That will need doing again!' he barked, as Ranjit finished mopping one end of the room. 'I can see streaks of mud.' Ranjit went to refill the bucket, and the colonel turned his attention to Ryan. 'You need to focus on the tiles near the floor,' he demanded, 'where the grime has built up.'

'I'm working my way down!' blurted out Ryan, frustrated. He was doing what he'd been told. The colonel had no right to criticise him.

'That's more like it,' sneered the colonel. 'That's more like the whiny Jacobs I expect. Give me twenty push-ups for talking back, right now.'

'But I was trying to explain...'

'Listen here, cadet. I am not interested in excuses. I'm interested in you doing as you're told. Do you understand me?'

Ryan remembered he'd promised his friends that he wouldn't let the colonel wind him up.

Fine job you're doing so far, Ryan.

'Yes, sir,' he said.

'So let's make that forty push-ups. If you fail, or answer me back again then I'll add another hour on to your cleaning duty. Begin.'

'Yes, sir.'

Ryan got down. The colonel stood so close that

Ryan's head practically hit the man's boots every time he did a push-up. It was hard work, but he did all forty without collapsing.

As he tried to get up, the colonel stopped him with his foot. 'You might as well stay down there and do the grimy tiles first, like I told you,' he said.

'Yes, sir,' replied Ryan, trying to keep his anger in. He picked up the brush and started spraying and scrubbing the mouldy grouting near the floor. The colonel stood over him for a while, before leaving him to his fate.

By now, Ryan was kneeling on the wet floor in the shower area, near the drain. The water had soaked through his trouser legs, making him cold and uncomfortable. He was spraying and scrubbing, trying to remove the black scum.

'And I thought I had it bad,' said Ranjit, as he looked in on Ryan, 'but man, that job *really* sucks.'

'Only eight and a half hours to go,' said Ryan, through gritted teeth. 'Let's hope that all the colonel's games aren't this much fun. I don't think I could handle it.'

Ranjit laughed. 'You're doing well, mate. Keep it up. He'll lay off you, eventually.'

'Think of me when you're playing pool,' said Ryan, wiping his forehead with his sleeve. 'Or when you're lying in on Saturday morning.'

'I will,' promised Ranjit. 'Don't worry. It'll be over before you know it.'

I hope so, thought Ryan.

He was wondering if Blackfell could really be any

worse than this.

18. SHATTERED

The cleaning dragged, and by the end of the week Ryan's hands were numb from scrubbing. Prefects often appeared to check on him, and they always found him hard at work. By lunchtime on Saturday, the showers gleamed, ready for the inspection.

'What do you call that?' demanded the colonel, pointing to one corner. 'Do it again.'

Ryan had been expecting it. The colonel wanted him to say something stupid, but he wasn't going to fall into that trap. He knelt down and got back to work.

For the next half hour, the colonel found fault, pointing out other areas that had been 'missed'. Ryan figured there was only one way through this, and that was to stay calm and do everything he was asked. Sure enough, after a while the colonel seemed to get bored.

'As I said before, Jacobs,' he said, 'even you have your uses. You're dismissed.'

'Thank you, sir,' said Ryan, feeling like he'd passed a test. Maybe now the colonel would get off his case?

The cleaning aside, his first week at Devonmoor had been an interesting mix of normal school life and unusual experiences. Lessons took place every weekday. Ordinary subjects were mixed with unusual ones such as emotional intelligence, military strategy, flying and engineering. One day a week he got to focus on the lesson of his choice: computing. An entire day spent in the ICT lab with Mr Davids studying hacking, programming, algorithms and firewalls. It was challenging stuff, but he loved it. He'd been in heaven as he lounged around in the futuristic basement chatting to the teacher and developing new code.

There were things about the academy that he hated. Drill was a drag, and he was getting sick of the dark grey uniform. Then there was the food. Ryan's haphazard attempts to answer the questions in the canteen tests had resulted in some pretty grim meals.

But he could cope with those things as long as he had decent mates. Things had got a lot better with the boys in his dorm: the others saw he was trying not to get them in trouble. Even Jael was being friendly. Ranjit and Ayana hung around a lot with their group, and Sparks seemed to like everyone.

To his surprise, Ryan no longer hated Devonmoor.

But the next night, everything changed.

***

It was 3.23am when it happened.

The window shattered, waking Ryan up with a start.

Dark figures scrambled into the room. Adrenaline kicked his brain into action and Ryan rolled out of the bottom bunk. His feet hardly touched the floor before one intruder had grabbed and spun him, slamming him face-first against the wall.

'Make any noise and your friend gets it,' the man hissed in Ryan's ear.

Within seconds, they wrapped thick industrial tape around his wrists, and sealed his mouth shut. He glanced to the side to see the same thing happening to Kev and Jael. Lee was slung over one man's shoulders, being carried out of the window in his underwear. He looked terrified.

From what Ryan could make out in the darkness, there were four assailants in total—adults dressed in black, faces covered with ski masks. He had been hoping that this was a schoolboy prank, but it all seemed too professional, too serious.

'Mmmmmm, mmmmm,' Ryan tried to shout through the tape, but it earned him a punch in the stomach. They dumped him on the floor next to the others and his feet were taped together.

Then, as suddenly as it had begun, the drama ended. The men exited through the window, leaving the boys alone.

Silence.

Ryan awkwardly manoeuvred himself onto his feet. He could barely see anything. Was anyone else in the school even aware of what had happened? Already Lee's captors would be heading out of the school grounds, and no-one was doing anything.

The rooms were always locked at night but Ryan leaned back and tried the handle, anyway. No luck.

He slammed his body into the door as hard as he could, trying to draw someone's attention.

Kev had got to his feet and jumped towards the small bathroom, turning on the light. It spilled out into the bedroom so they could see.

The three lads looked at each other. No-one seemed to be injured but all of them had tape around their mouth, hands and feet. Moving was difficult. Talking was impossible.

Kev had a plan. He shuffled his way towards the window. Ryan guessed what he hoped to do: cut the tape on the broken shards.

It might have worked if he had been wearing shoes, but as Kev got closer, his face screwed up with pain. He fell backwards, his feet cut to shreds by the sharp slivers of glass, the tiles smeared with blood. Fighting back tears, Kev shook his head: *it's not going to work*.

There had to be another way out of this.

After a minute or two, Ryan had an idea of his own. He lowered himself to the floor. With his back to Jael, Ryan felt for the tape around the boy's wrists. Once he found the end, he pulled on it, unwinding it until the other boy could pull his hands apart.

Jael ripped the tape from his mouth and started freeing the other lads.

'Who the hell were they?' exclaimed Ryan.

'No idea.' Jael looked scared. Even at Devonmoor, this was far from normal.

The door burst open, and the lights flickered on. Dr Fleur stood there, looking furious.

'*What* is going on?' she demanded.

'They took Lee!' exclaimed Jael, 'and Kev is injured!'

She looked at the lads, at the discarded industrial tape and the smashed window, and she seemed to perform a quick mental calculation. She snapped her fingers twice and two soldiers appeared from the corridor, ready to take orders.

'Arrange a complete lockdown, code Alpha,' she said.

The soldiers ran off, one of them repeating the order into a comms device.

'You boys come with me.'

'But ma'am,' said Jael, 'Kev can't walk.'

'Well, in that case you'd better carry him.' She turned and strode down the corridor.

Jael rolled his eyes and moved alongside Kev. Ryan took his place on the other side.

'On three,' said Jael. 'One, two, three.'

They lifted Kev and—given that he was bigger than either of them—they half-carried, half-dragged him down the quiet corridor towards the medical room.

***

While Dr Fleur offered little in the way of sympathy, she dealt efficiently with the wounds. Kev bit down hard on a piece of leather as she removed the slivers of glass with a pair of tweezers. He didn't complain, even thanking her when she finished.

'You'll need to stay here for a day or two to allow the wounds to heal,' instructed Dr Fleur. 'We have to make sure the cuts don't get infected.' Kev looked disappointed, but nodded.

'Dr Fleur, have you heard anything?' asked Ryan. 'Have they found Lee?'

'No, they haven't been able to locate him.' Dr Fleur busied herself with tidying up the first aid kit. 'That's all I know.'

'It doesn't make sense,' Jael said. 'Why would anyone want to kidnap him?'

'It's not like his family are rich or anything,' added Kev. 'He's one of the poorest people here. They won't get a ransom.'

'Perhaps they need a pilot?' suggested Ryan.

'Maybe,' allowed Jael. 'But there are a lot easier ways to get a pilot than breaking into a top-secret boarding school and kidnapping one.'

Ryan could see his point. 'Do you think it has anything to do with the former student? The Outlier?'

'Possibly,' allowed Kev, 'but I still don't know why he'd need Lee.'

Just then Dr Torren arrived.

'Sir, what's happening?' asked Jael.

'I'm afraid I have nothing to tell you,' he said. 'I know how close you are to Lee, and I can assure you that the army and the school have their best people working on this.'

'Did you get the guys on camera?' asked Ryan.

'No, the security system seems to have malfunctioned. The intruders knew what they were doing. These were not amateurs. I need to find out what happened. Every single detail. Who's going to start?'

Jael described what had taken place, with Kev and Ryan sometimes interrupting, adding their own details. But as they told their story, Ryan realised there wasn't much that would identify the kidnappers. Dr Torren soon reached the same conclusion.

'What happens now?' asked Ryan.

'You and Jael need to go back to your dormitory. You mustn't tell anyone about this.'

'What?' asked Jael, forgetting all protocol. 'You want us to keep it a secret? Why?'

'I know it's difficult,' soothed Dr Torren, 'but it would cause widespread panic. If anyone asks you about Lee, you need to say that he's here in the medical room. The official story will be that there was a fight, a serious fight, during which the window got broken and Lee and Kev both got hurt.'

'I'd never fight Lee!' pointed out Kev. 'No-one is going to believe that!'

Dr Torren considered that for a moment. 'No, you might be right. But if we say that Ryan caused it then the whole story becomes plausible.'

'No way, sir!' objected Jael. 'That's not true!'

'Why do I get the blame?' whined Ryan. 'People already think I'm bad news. No-one will be friends with me if they find out I put Lee and Kev in the hospital wing!'

'Cadets!' Dr Torren said, his tone sharp. 'You seem to be forgetting your place. You *will* tell people that's what happened. It's a direct order.'

There was a brief pause and then Jael backed down. 'Yes, sir.' He knew better than to contradict a teacher. He dropped back into his chair.

Ryan stayed on his feet. He glared at Dr Torren. 'Everyone's gonna hate me.'

'Maybe, but they'll soon forgive you when they find out the truth. Hopefully, we won't have to cover it up for long.'

Ryan was too tired to argue. 'Fine,' he sighed, 'whatever. Feel free to drag my reputation through the mud.'

'Good. That's settled then.'

'Can we at least go back to bed now?' asked Jael.

'Yes,' said Dr Torren. 'You might as well get another couple of hours sleep before lessons.'

'You can't expect us to go to classes today!'

'On the contrary, I do expect it,' said the teacher.

Ryan shook his head in disbelief but for once he didn't argue. There was no point. He'd learned that much.

They trudged back to the dorm. The window had already been fixed, the broken glass swept up, the blood-stains washed off the tiles. The cover-up had begun.

Ryan and Jael fell into their beds, exhausted. They'd hardly shut their eyes before the siren announced it was time for drill.

19. ULTIMATUM

'Cadet Jacobs.' The voice was quiet, and barely registered in Ryan's brain. It seemed distant.

He ignored it.

'JACOBS!'

It wasn't quiet any longer. Someone was shouting at close range.

Ryan jerked awake.

The science teacher, Mr Cho, was in his face, looking angry.

'Are we disturbing you?' he asked.

'Yes, sir. I mean no, sir. Sorry sir, I'm exhausted.' Ryan could hear some cadets sniggering behind him.

'That may be true but sleeping through lessons is not the solution.' The teacher moved away. 'Try to stay awake! We have a lot to cover and you're already way behind everyone else as it is.'

Ryan hadn't been able to keep his eyes open all morning. Even when he was awake, he couldn't focus. The events of the night before kept playing on his mind. *Where was Lee? What had happened to him? Was he alive?*

He couldn't get out of the classroom fast enough when they were dismissed. He started making his way towards the canteen.

But he never made it.

Turning the corner, he walked into James Sarrell. Before Ryan could slip past, Sarrell had grabbed him by the collar and started dragging him down the corridor. Ryan tried to pull away, but the boy's grip was too tight.

'If you want to see Lee again, then come with me.'

Ryan stopped struggling, as much from shock as from obedience. A few of his classmates passed and shot meaningful glances at him but didn't get involved. This wasn't their fight. Besides, they'd heard what Ryan had done to Lee and Kev, so as far as they were concerned he deserved a beating. Ryan would have to handle this on his own.

Sarrell pushed him into a large store cupboard and slipped in behind him before closing the door. A low-energy bulb lit the gloomy interior.

'Listen up, Jacobs,' said Sarrell. 'Don't make a sound or try to fight me. Your friend's life depends on it.'

'What? Where is he? What have you done with him?'

Sarrell punched him hard in the stomach and Ryan doubled over, banging his head on a shelf. 'Which part of not making a sound do you not understand? I'll do the talking. You stay quiet.' He leaned down; his mouth close to Ryan's ear. 'Your friend is being held captive. The men that have him want something from you, and unless you deliver it to them, they will kill him. Do you understand?'

Ryan nearly spoke again but, seeing Sarrell

135

clench his fist, he nodded.

'Good boy,' continued Sarrell. 'Here's what you're going to do. You need to hack into the army server and extract any files linked to Project Leopard on to a memory stick. Then deliver it to a car which will be waiting for you at the gates of the school tonight. It will be there at nine.'

'But it's not possible...' Ryan started. Sarrell punched him again, dropping him to his knees.

'The people I work for are not interested in your excuses. It's simple. Either they get the file tonight or your friend dies. Don't even think of telling anyone of this little encounter. You mention it to anyone, *anyone*, and that's the last you'll ever see of Lee.'

Sarrell let that sink in. 'Now, take off your jacket.'

Ryan somehow removed his military jacket in the cramped space, trembling with anger and fear. Sarrell took off his own jacket and swapped it with Ryan's.

'Wear this. It's bugged so we hear everything you say. You should also know that one of our agents works for the school as part of the security team. If they see anything suspicious on camera, then Lee will pay for it.'

Ryan gulped and tugged on the jacket. As he zipped it up he could feel a strange lump in the lining.

'I'm warning you Jacobs,' hissed Sarrell, 'you may think you're a genius but from this moment on, we own you. Talk to anyone, your friend dies. Fail to deliver the file, your friend dies.' Grabbing Ryan by the throat, Sarrell lifted him off his feet and pressed him hard against the shelves. 'Project Leopard. Nine o'clock tonight at the gates. Do you understand everything I've told you?'

Ryan nodded.

Sarrell released his grip and Ryan gasped for air, expecting another punch in the stomach. Instead, Sarrell ruffled his hair and grinned. 'Good luck, Jacobs. And remember, we'll be watching you.'

With that, Sarrell slipped out of the store cupboard, closing the door on Ryan, who collapsed to the floor.

This was bad.

This was really bad.

He wasn't sure if he could get the files for Project Leopard in time. There was every chance he'd get caught trying.

Could he tell? If so, then who? He didn't know who he could trust. Lee's life was too important. Whoever was behind this knew what they were doing.

For now, at least, Sarrell was right.

They owned him. He had to do whatever they said.

**

The computer lab was dark and empty, lit by a few spotlights. That suited Ryan, who always worked in the shadows. He made his way over to his favourite terminal in the corner, having wolfed down his food at lunch. He was cutting it fine as it was.

His stomach tensed as he logged on. The last time he'd gained access to the Ministry of Defence server, his 'mites' program had allowed the army to trace him. This time he couldn't allow that to happen. If it did, they might catch him before he made it to the school gates. And even if they caught him after that, he'd get expelled. The only solution was to make sure they didn't trace him at all, and that meant finding out where he had gone wrong.

Calling up the program code, he checked it line by line. What would allow the army to identify the true source of the hack? Time ticked away and Ryan started to sweat. It had taken days to put this algorithm together. He'd never fix it in a few hours.

He was close to tears when Mr Davids strolled into the lab, whistling.

'Ah, Ryan,' he said. 'Hard at work I see, yes? What are you working on, my boy?'

Ryan hesitated. 'I'm trying to work out how you traced the mites program,' he admitted, deciding to take a risk, 'but I can't see how. The code attacks from several hundred different locations. There's no way that anyone should be able to trace the source.'

If Mr Davids was suspicious, he didn't show it. Fascinated as he was with his subject, it seemed a natural question for Ryan to ask.

'Think about it,' he said, perching on the desk opposite. 'The code is identical in every program, yes?'

'Yes, sir. Even the destination for the hacked data is remote. There's no way to trace the source.'

'A difficult problem indeed.' Mr Davids had a twinkle in his eye. 'What could tell them apart? To the server they look like identical attacks.'

'I don't get it! It can't be done!'

Mr Davids laughed. 'I love your passion, my boy,' he said. 'You'll work it out. The simplest solutions are often the ones we find it hardest to spot. Think FIFO.'

'FIFO?' Ryan mulled it over in his head. FIFO meant 'First In, First Out', like a giant queue of data being dealt with in order. It had nothing to do with the mites program at all.

Or did it?

The pieces fell into place.

'The source of the hack is the first piece of code to hit?' he half-asked, half-told the teacher. 'It gets there before the others. So the first one to register is the one you trace?'

'There you go! It's so simple!' Mr Davids rubbed his hands in excitement. 'It's a matter of a thousandth of a nanosecond, less than that, but it's all recorded in a list in the computer's memory. If you can access the list, then you can find the hacker.'

'Genius,' muttered Ryan.

'And if you find the hacker, you may get a new student at your school!' joked Mr Davids, heading off into his office and chuckling to himself.

All Ryan needed to do was off-set the timing so the actual source of the hack wasn't the first of the mites to hit the MOD server. That shouldn't be too hard.

Mr Davids popped back out of his office a few moments later. 'While I appreciate your commitment, Ryan,' he said, 'shouldn't you be in lessons right now?'

Ryan checked the time. It was 1.33pm. He was

running late for his next class.

Cursing under his breath, he logged off as fast as he could and sprinted out of the lab.

***

He knew he was in trouble the moment he opened the classroom door.

'Cadet Jacobs, do come in.' Mrs Tracey did not sound happy.

'I'm sorry I'm late, ma'am. I lost track of time.'

'That is not acceptable, cadet. You will report back here at four o'clock and we'll see if we can encourage you to be punctual in future. Take a seat.'

'Yes, ma'am.' It was all Ryan could do to stop himself protesting, but he knew that he'd just make things worse. How could he explain to the teacher that he didn't have time for a detention because he was trying to save Lee's life?

The small lump in his jacket pressed against his chest. He couldn't say anything. He just had to hope she didn't make him stay too long and that he had enough time left for the hack. As if he wasn't under enough pressure as it was.

It was a stupid mistake to make, and he couldn't afford to make mistakes like that right now. Lee's life hung in the balance.

The longer the lesson went on, the more Ryan's frustration and worry grew.

Time was running out.

20. FRUSTRATION

3.59pm.

Ryan stood at the door to Mrs Tracey's room and knocked.

He'd considered not showing up. He didn't care if he got into worse trouble—he could handle that. But if the prefects started searching the school for him, then things would go from bad to worse.

'Enter.'

Ryan walked in and stood to attention, waiting for the teacher to look up.

'Ah, Cadet Jacobs.' she said, eventually. 'Take a seat.'

Ryan sat at a desk in the front row.

'Punctuality is important to me,' she explained, in a matter-of-fact way. 'So if you are late to my lesson, even by a minute, you will receive a detention.'

'Yes, ma'am.'

'How long you stay here is up to you.' She placed a piece of paper on the desk in front of him. 'When you've answered these correctly, you can leave.'

Ryan scanned the sheet. It had fifteen questions on it, all difficult algebra problems. But he was good at maths. He could do this.

'You may begin.'

The first few were pretty straightforward, and Ryan whizzed through them. Maybe he could be out in twenty minutes?

But the further down the sheet Ryan got, the harder the problems were and the slower his brain became. He was still tired, and he made stupid mistakes. Time was ticking away; precious minutes that Lee's life depended on.

Think, Ryan, think!

It took him over half an hour to answer all the questions except one. He couldn't crack it. He remembered something about how to expand multiple nested brackets but his brain was fried. After a few abortive attempts, he raised his hand.

'Yes?' asked Mrs Tracey. 'Have you finished?'

'Almost, ma'am,' admitted Ryan. 'I'm stuck on problem fourteen. I can't do it.'

'I see,' said the teacher, walking over to take a look. 'Well, your other answers look good. You should be able to solve question fourteen by now.'

'But I can't,' protested Ryan. 'I've tried.'

'That may be the case. But if you could do it, you would be leaving now. Whereas if you can't do it, you will be here until five o'clock. Want to give it another go?'

Ryan felt sick as he saw the time slipping away. It was already 4.34pm.

'I'll try, ma'am.'

Holding his head, he frowned as he took another look at the figures.

Take it step by step, he told himself. *Don't panic.*

Ten minutes and several failed attempts later, he had a breakthrough. By multiplying the numbers out, he could cancel out the first set of brackets. Now, a quick bit of mental arithmetic meant he could whittle the complex fractions down to a simple solution.

'Mrs Tracey,' he said, looking up.

'Yes?'

'I think I've solved it, ma'am,' said Ryan, glancing at the clock. He needed to get going. She walked over to him and checked his result.

'Well done,' she said. 'It seems you could do it after all.'

Ryan's body tensed like a coiled spring, desperate for her to let him loose.

'And you understand why you had a detention today?' she asked, driving the point home.

'Because I was late, ma'am,' said Ryan, trying to keep any sense of impatience out of his voice. He knew how teachers worked. If he let her know how keen he was to leave, she'd keep him there for longer.

'Correct. Don't be late to my lesson again. You can go.'

She'd hardly finished the sentence before Ryan was out the room and careering down the corridor.

***

His boots clattered on the tiled floor as he flew down the basement steps towards the ICT lab. At the bottom, he collided with someone coming out of the classroom.

Not just someone.

Sarah Devonmoor.

The books and papers she was holding flew in all directions as she fell against the wall. 'What the—'

Initial shock turned to annoyance as she regained her balance. 'Cadet Jacobs, what's the hurry?' she demanded.

'I-I-I'm sorry...' stuttered Ryan. He knelt down to pick the stuff up.

'On your feet, cadet!' ordered Sarah. 'You stand to attention and salute when you pass a prefect.'

Ryan dropped the papers and did as he was told.

'Cadet, are you aware that running in the corridor is a breach of the academy rules?' she asked.

'Yes, ma'am.' Ryan tried to sound polite and apologetic, but it just came out sounding feeble.

'So you must have an excellent reason for breaking those rules?'

'No, ma'am.' What else could he say?

Sarah looked at him like he was a cockroach she was about to crush underfoot. 'Well, then, as you are so keen on running, you will volunteer for the cross-country team. I expect to see your name on the sign-up sheet by tomorrow lunchtime. Do I make myself clear?'

Cross-country running was Ryan's idea of hell, but he guessed that she already knew that. At this precise moment, though, Ryan couldn't see past the next few hours. If he survived tonight and avoided being expelled from Devonmoor, then extra cross-country might sound like a threat. Right now it barely registered.

'Yes, ma'am.'

'Good. *Now* you can pick up my books.'

Ryan crouched down to gather up everything she had dropped. He handed it to her, embarrassed.

'In future, watch where you're going.' The prefect turned and strode away.

What was her problem with him?

Come on, Ryan, he told himself. *You don't have time for this.*

He couldn't get distracted by Sarah Devonmoor, whatever the deal was.

He had to save Lee.

***

After the stress and confusion of the afternoon, the dark interior of the lab was comforting: the subdued spotlights, the smell of warm electronics, the gentle hum of computers. It wasn't empty: a few other cadets were working, but they seemed engrossed in what they were doing. Ryan sat down and got to work.

He had an hour before things got tricky. Dinner was at 6.00pm and he had to be there. The plan was simple: finish the algorithm now, then eat, and execute the code afterwards. The hack would take an hour, but he would need good, uninterrupted time and it wasn't easy to know if anyone would be around. Mr Davids was his biggest worry—the over-enthusiastic teacher might take too much interest in what his favourite student was up to.

And hacking wasn't always predictable—it could take longer. There were usually things you hadn't thought of. Ryan tried not to dwell on that.

'Mites' wasn't a sophisticated enough program to prevent the army from knowing they were under attack. Its strength lay in the pure quantity of problems it presented the defence system with. Being hacked from hundreds of locations confused and overloaded the normal defence protocols. While they sorted the mess out and tried to untangle the knot their firewall was in, Ryan would locate and retrieve the Project Leopard files.

Soon, Ryan was in the zone. His fingers shot across the keys so quickly they became a blur. His eyes never left the screen. The code he was creating was basic but effective. It should stop Ryan's terminal from being the first to connect with the server and prevent them from tracing him.

Somehow, he finished it within the hour. He couldn't get cocky; he still needed to check it. This had to be perfect. If the program didn't work, then it was game over.

But this wasn't a game.

And this time Ryan wouldn't get arrested.

This time Lee would die.

No pressure, he thought to himself, trying to push several grotesque images of Lee's demise from his brain. *Don't screw this up, Ryan, don't screw this up.*

So far, everything was going to plan. The code

was ready, but it was nearly six.

He logged off and headed to the canteen.

21. CHOICES

Ryan pushed his food around the plate. He was too nervous to eat: there was still loads to do, and he needed to be back in the lab. But dinner was a formal affair at the academy. Everyone arrived at the same time and ate together. You didn't get to leave early.

There were no canteen tests in the evenings and the food was good. Ryan knew he would focus better if he could stomach it. He worked his way through the chicken and chips one mouthful at a time, forcing it down.

Ranjit sat opposite him. He clearly knew that Ryan was lying to him about the events of the previous night. 'So you're saying that Kev started on you?' he asked for the third time.

'Yeah, I already said. We were arguing, and he snapped and came at me. I tried to fight him off. Then Lee joined in. I pushed them back and Kev fell straight into the window and broke it.'

'What was the argument about?' Ranjit focused intently on Ryan.

'I wouldn't clean my boots, and they said they're getting sick of getting in trouble because of me.'

There was at least a grain of truth in that. Ryan had straightened out his cover story. He felt guilty for lying to everyone, but if anyone found out the truth, then the teachers would know that the leak came from him or Jael.

'That's insane,' said Ranjit. 'I've never seen either of them lose their temper like that.'

'Well,' said Ryan, 'none of us expected it to get so serious. Kev landed on the window and that was it—broken glass everywhere.'

'So how come you weren't punished?'

'I was,' countered Ryan, trying to think up a convincing answer. 'I mean, I haven't been yet, but I will be. I have to report to the colonel later and he's got something brutal in mind. He wanted me to sweat it out. I don't want to think about what that's going to involve, to be honest.'

Ranjit looked thoughtful and stayed silent during dessert. Ryan was relieved. He tried to not catch anyone else's eye while he ate his chocolate cake. Lying was hard work, and his thoughts needed to be elsewhere. He watched the clock, eager to escape the moment they were dismissed.

One of the prefects, Lara O'Connell, stood up, and the room fell silent. 'A reminder, cadets, that science exams will take place on Monday and anyone scoring less than ninety percent will be banned from the common room for a week.' There was a muffled groan from the students. 'Dormitory fourteen, you're on clear up this evening. Everyone else, dismissed.'

Ryan got up from the table and pushed his way towards the door with the others. The noise in the dining room was deafening as people made their way out. As he was leaving, a hand grabbed his shoulder.

'Not so fast, Ryan.' It was Jael.

'What?' asked Ryan, confused.

'Dormitory fourteen? That's us. We're on clean-up. I hope you didn't have anything planned for the next few hours.'

'Clean-up?' Ryan scanned the dining room where almost a hundred students had left dirty plates, cutlery and glasses. Chicken bones and chocolate crumbs were scattered around like debris.

'That's right, man,' Jael said. 'See all of this? We get the joyous privilege of washing it up. The dorms take it in turns and tonight it's our turn.'

'But we don't have Lee and Kev! It'll take twice as long!'

'Well, you could try raising that with the colonel if you like?' suggested Jael, 'but I don't think he'll cry. Come on, the quicker we get going, the quicker it will be done.'

Ryan allowed Jael to lead him into the industrial kitchen where dirty pots and pans were piled high. It was deserted. Two giant sinks with metal draining boards sat ominously along one wall.

'You fill the sinks and I'll start collecting the plates,' Jael directed.

'But Jael, I can't do this tonight.'

'It's not like we have a choice. It's how things work here.'

Ryan edged towards the door. 'Look, I'm sorry. There's something I have to do. I need to leave. Now.'

'You can't,' said Jael. 'It's against the rules.'

'I don't care about the stupid rules!'

'You're not leaving me to do this alone.' Jael sounded desperate. 'You step out of here and I'm going straight to the colonel.'

'Well, good luck with that. The way I figure it, if you do then the whole dormitory gets into trouble, right? You'd get punished as well.' It was a bluff, but it worked.

'What's got into you?' There was desperation in Jael's eyes. 'If we don't get this done, we'll be on clear up for the rest of term. All of us!'

'You better get on with it then,' shrugged Ryan, trying to appear unconcerned. 'I don't care.'

'I thought we were friends! You promised you wouldn't get us into any more trouble. You said you'd try to follow the rules. Or was that all a lie?'

'Seriously,' countered Ryan, 'do you ever stop whining?'

Jael swore and lunged at him.

Ryan wasn't sure if Jael was trying to grab him or hit him, but he didn't give him the chance to do either. He reacted fast, dodging to the side and pushing the boy backwards.

Jael fell, his flailing arm catching a pile of dirty plates and bringing them crashing down on top of him. He ended up half-sitting, half-lying on the floor, his uniform smeared with cold gravy.

'Sorry,' said Ryan, backing away, 'but I have to go.'

Jael climbed to his feet and brushed small pieces of chicken off his jacket. 'That's great,' he said, 'just great. Thanks for being such a good mate.'

Ryan slipped out of the kitchen leaving Jael angry and alone. He couldn't deal with that right now. Hopefully, at some point he'd be able to explain his actions.

If Jael ever let him explain.

And if Ryan got the opportunity to tell him.

***

At least the lab was empty.

Settling himself down, Ryan ran his hands through his fringe and prepared himself while the machine logged on.

'Here goes nothing,' he muttered, and then felt self-conscious as he remembered the kidnappers could hear everything he said.

He accessed his hidden website with his virtual storeroom of hacking tools and downloaded the kit. After double-checking the settings, he activated 'Spider's Web' which would create the initial connections with hundreds of other computers around the world, the locations the mites would attack from. Once that was up and running, it was down to the mites to do their thing.

With a sense of déjà vu, he typed in the digital address of the main MOD server. Everything seemed so calm, like it had on that fateful night when he'd last tried to hack into the system. He guiltily remembered his promise to Lady Devonmoor that he would never do this again. He'd meant it. And yet here he was, doing exactly that.

He typed the command into the prompt box: "Run mites.exe".

'I'm hacking into the server now,' he said, for the benefit of whoever was listening. If this all went wrong, then at least Lee's kidnappers would know he had tried. Ryan hoped that would be enough.

The next few minutes passed slowly as Ryan waited while the software did its thing. The noise of approaching footsteps disturbed him. Now was not a good time to be interrupted. He had two options: hide or act normal.

Acting normal would have been the obvious choice but if Jael had been annoyed enough to report him, then someone could be coming to accost him in the lab. He couldn't risk it. He switched the monitor off and dived under the desk.

The door to the lab opened and Ryan recognised the cheerful whistle of Mr Davids. It was unlikely that the teacher knew anything about Ryan skiving kitchen duty, but it would be awkward to appear from under the desk now, and even trickier to answer any of his questions if he took an interest in what Ryan was working on. So Ryan stayed huddled where he was, hoping that Mr Davids wasn't planning to stay. The teacher sat down at his own terminal, oblivious to Ryan's presence.

Minutes ticked by.

Ryan tried to come up with a plan. By now the mites program should have cracked the Ministry of Defence firewall, and it wouldn't take them long to discover the attack and to defend their servers. Ryan had to act fast: this was no time to be crammed under a table.

As he was about to clamber out with a weak excuse, Ryan heard the door open and a voice that sent shivers down his spine. It was James Sarrell.

'Mr Davids, sir?'

'Yes, yes... err, relax cadet. At ease or whatever.' Ryan smiled to himself. The computing teacher didn't fit in well at the military academy. 'What is it?'

'Colonel Keller is having trouble with his computer, sir. He requests your immediate assistance.'

'Very well,' said Mr Davids, standing up. 'I guess it won't do to keep the colonel waiting. I suppose he has checked that the thing's plugged in...?'

As they left, Ryan jumped up and switched the monitor back on. That was a lucky break.

The words were right there, where they should be: 'Ministry of Defence Secure System'. He breathed a sigh of relief. Now to find Project Leopard before anyone traced him. Activating the 'hunter' application, Ryan could locate the files in a matter of seconds.

He downloaded them to his terminal and then evacuated the mites, leaving a harmless virus in the system. He hoped the army would think that's why they were hacked and they wouldn't notice anything about Project Leopard until it was much too late.

He'd done it.

Making a backup of the files on the memory stick, Ryan glanced at the clock. 8.11pm. He had a little spare time: enough to see what was in the files.

'I'm finding the Project Leopard files now,' he lied,

for the benefit of Lee's captors. He didn't want them getting suspicious. As he opened the first file and scanned the contents, he wished he hadn't. Whatever Leopard was, it wasn't anything that someone evil should have access to. The diagram and specifications were way out of his league, but he knew he was looking at a weapon. Probably a super-weapon. Maybe chemical or nuclear.

If he let these plans get into the wrong hands, then hundreds of people could die. Or thousands. Millions even.

But if he didn't hand them over, then they'd kill Lee.

His brain was working slowly; much too slowly.

There was no way out. He had to decide between rescuing his friend and putting thousands of others at risk. Ryan's stomach tensed as he thought about the choice he was being forced to make.

Whatever he did, people would die.

And it would all be his fault.

22. DITCH

8.47pm.

The boys' toilets were deserted. Ryan clutched at the memory stick. It was raining outside, so he'd wrapped it in a small clear plastic bag he'd found in Mr Davids' office.

Locking himself in a cubicle, he climbed onto a toilet seat and then up onto the cistern, reaching up to the window. He pushed it open as far as it would go, wishing it was nearer to the ground. This had to be the best way out of the academy as there were no cameras in the toilets whereas all the fire exits were alarmed.

He poked his head out of the opening to check where he would land. It was pitch black out there, and the rain bounced off the tarmac. The storm would make it hard to see, but it would also provide some cover.

Here goes nothing. He pushed himself through, clumsily dropping to the ground. It seemed he hadn't got any better at climbing out of windows since his arrest.

The rain hammered down, soaking his clothes. He was going to get drenched, and it was pointless trying to prevent it, so he stopped hunching over and stood up. A rush of adrenaline coursed through him, giving him a warm sensation despite the downpour.

He skirted round the edge of the building in the darkness, ducking past the windows. As he reached the kitchen block, he could see Jael through the steamed-up glass, standing at the sink surrounded by stacks of plates.

Ryan hurried on, passing the front of the Academy. The offices were there: Lady Devonmoor's room, the grand entrance hall, the boardroom. Light streamed from the windows out onto the garden, taunting Ryan with the promise of a warm, dry welcome inside the school if he just abandoned all hopes of rescuing Lee.

It wasn't going to happen. He turned and faced the other direction, shielding his eyes from the heavy rain with his hand. He forced himself forward, fighting the wind. It was as if nature itself was trying to stop him.

Checking that no guards were around, Ryan sprinted across the front lawn. As he neared the bushes on the far side, he heard someone approaching down the driveway and he skidded to a halt. A soldier emerged from the trees, heading in his direction. He had a large Alsatian dog on a lead, its nose to the floor. The animal might have appeared menacing, but in the rain it looked forlorn and dejected.

'This is Cobra Two Zero reporting. All clear at the front of the building,' the soldier shouted into his comms device. He hadn't seen Ryan yet, but all he needed to do was look up. 'THIS IS COBRA TWO

ZERO. DO YOU READ ME?' The soldier shouted louder this time, sounding annoyed. He turned to shelter the device from the wind, giving Ryan precious seconds to find a hiding place.

Ryan threw himself into a prickly bush at the edge of the lawn, crouching out of sight. He held his breath, hoping that neither the dog nor the man had heard the sudden movement.

He was in luck. The soldier passed by without glancing in his direction, keen to finish his rounds and get out of the rain.

Once he was sure that they had gone, Ryan tried to extract himself from the bush. It wasn't as easy as he expected. Thorns scratched at his hands and face, and his jacket tore as he tried to get free.

Great way to spend the evening, Ryan, he thought to himself, as he rubbed the cuts on his arms.

Beyond the neat front garden, woodland surrounded the driveway. The shadows on the road made it hard to see. Despite that, he broke into a light jog. He needed to keep himself warm, and he had no idea how far it was to the front gate. He had to make it in time. His soaking-wet uniform felt heavy against his skin and his face stung where the thorns had scratched him. He pushed the discomfort to the back of his mind. It wasn't helping.

The road seemed to go on and on, and he started to panic. Where was the gate? What if he was going the wrong way, and he'd missed a turn? He picked up his pace, running as fast as he dared, then tripped up a bump in the road and flew forwards, landing on the wet tarmac. He climbed back to his feet, his hands and knees grazed, his wrist throbbing.

As he started moving again, he could see headlights in the distance coming towards him. Could this be the men that he was supposed to meet? Or was it someone else driving towards the school? Lee's captors weren't likely to come into the grounds.

Ryan looked for cover. There were no hedges nearby and the tree trunks were too thin. There was only one place to hide: a deep ditch running along the side of the road. He dived into it, lying flat as the car drew closer.

He smelt it first, and then felt it soaking into every part of his clothing: his uniform filling with cold, stagnant mud. He hadn't realised how deep the ditch was, but he had to remain as still and low as he could. There was nothing he could do but let it happen.

It's just mud, he told himself, trying to ignore the smell of something much worse. It made him want to throw up.

Once the car had passed, Ryan climbed out, the mud dripping off him, his hair lank and disgusting. He was glad he'd wrapped the memory stick in a plastic bag else it would never survive.

He stumbled on. The rain was relentless.

Ryan was tired and could taste metal in his throat. He'd lost track of time and worried that he'd overshot the nine o'clock deadline. How long had he been out here?

'I'm nearly there,' he shouted, hoping that Lee's captors could hear him. 'I have what you want! Don't kill him!'

It was so dark that he almost ran headlong into the iron bars of the school gates. They were at least ten foot high. He wouldn't be able to climb over.

'I don't know if you can hear me,' he said into his jacket, 'but I'm at the gates with the memory stick.'

Nothing.

No response.

There was a flash of lightning, and then a peal of thunder. Ryan shivered, wondering what to do.

'I said I'm here!' he shouted again, slamming his fists hard against the iron bars in frustration. 'Are you coming or not?'

A car's headlights suddenly lit up the road on the other side and a dark vehicle drew closer. A man dressed in black got out and walked up to the gates, a ski-mask covering his face.

'Where's Lee?' Ryan shouted over the wind.

'He's safe. Hand over the data.'

'Not until you let him go.'

'If you don't hand it over, he will die.' It was the calm tone that scared Ryan the most.

'No, I have to see Lee!'

'Don't be stupid. As long as we get the files, we will release your friend.'

'Why should I believe you?' yelled Ryan, clutching the memory stick. There was the faint sound of a dog barking nearby.

'You hear that?' said the man. 'That's one of the guard dogs. They've picked up your scent. They'll be here any second. Give me the data, boy, or you'll never see your friend again.'

Ryan, defeated, let the man prise the memory stick out of his hand, between the bars of the gate. He watched as the man ran back to the car and got in.

There was no sign of Lee. No more instructions.

The car drove off into the distance.

And the rain kept falling.

23. CAUGHT

Ryan stumbled back along the road, dumping his jacket in the ditch. He couldn't stand to wear it a moment longer: the bug was inside it, and now it was soaking wet it offered little protection against the cold.

Behind him he could hear the dog—much closer this time. It was catching up. He wondered if it was on a lead or whether it was running free. Either way, he didn't have long.

He jumped into the ditch at the roadside and tried to run along it, hoping that it might throw them off the scent. The thick mud sucked his feet under as he splashed forward, saturating the thick socks and filling his boots with muck. It was slowing him down way too much, so he scrambled back out and headed into the woods.

He needed to find a place to hide—and fast.

His boots squelched as he staggered on. He desperately looked up at branches which were way beyond his reach. Behind him, the soldier's flashlight swept through the trees.

Ryan considered giving up, but that wasn't his style. If they wanted to take him, they'd have to do it by force. Besides, he could see strange dark shapes up ahead, and it gave him hope. Maybe he could find a hiding place after all. He stumbled forwards into a clearing. It was then that he figured out where he was: the assault course.

It looked creepy in the dark. He could make out tyres hanging from ropes on his left. That meant the climbing wall was on his right. And straight ahead? Straight ahead were the tunnels—the tiny, cramped tunnels that he'd blacked out in. And the only realistic hiding place.

Ryan cursed as he realised the cruel trick that fate had played on him. Just when he'd thought the worst was over, he had another impossible choice to make.

Would he allow himself to get caught and expelled, taken to a horrible boot camp where the days were filled with cold showers and long marches in the rain? Or would he face his worst fears and climb into the cramped, oppressive tunnels alone and in total darkness?

He wouldn't have to be in the tunnel for long, he reasoned, only until the soldier had gone. It had to be the better option. He edged towards the entrance, knelt down and looked in. Pitch black. Even darker than the woods.

He forced himself to feel the cold edge. The hole was smaller than he remembered it. What if he got trapped with no-one to help him? What if the tunnel collapsed while he was inside, and it crushed him? He retched at the thought and realised that he was kidding himself. It didn't matter what they did to him. He'd never be able to do it.

Standing back up, he saw the light approaching

through the trees. The dog was barking again. They were on his tail. Ryan splashed through a deep puddle and ran to a hanging rope, trying to pull himself up. Maybe he could get high enough to be out of sight?

It was a stupid plan, and he'd left it too late. He heard a noise in the bushes and glanced back. The Alsatian was running full speed towards him, its jaws wide open. In an awful moment of realisation, Ryan knew he wouldn't make it.

The dog clamped its teeth onto Ryan's lower leg and he cried out—a shout of pure terror—as he fell from the rope. He landed in wet mud and the beast leapt onto his chest. Ryan thought it was going to kill him; he closed his eyes and waited for it to tear at his throat.

'Don't move!' The shout came from the bushes. Ryan could see the soldier standing there.

'Help me,' he pleaded, staring into the slavering jaws of the Alsatian.

The soldier whistled, and the dog took a few steps back, growling. 'Do exactly as I say. Roll onto your front and put your hands behind your head.'

Ryan didn't need telling twice. The soldier knelt down, took hold of his arms and cuffed them behind his back.

Then the man hauled Ryan to his feet and twisted him around. 'Well, lad, I'm guessing you have a good excuse for being out in the grounds this late at night?' he asked.

'Not really,' admitted Ryan.

'Then you need to think of one,' suggested the soldier, 'else Colonel Keller is going to make mincemeat out of you.'

Ryan knew the soldier was right, but he was too tired and in too much pain to care. He limped along, his leg feeling numb where the dog had bitten it.

It was all over. He'd done what he had to do.

The rain didn't let up as they made their way back to the academy, but Ryan didn't mind. It hid the tears that streamed down his face, the mixture of fear, exhaustion and his anxiety about Lee pouring out.

The guard marched him up the front steps and into the entrance hall. The colonel and Dr Torren were standing talking to each other.

'What on earth?' Dr Torren exclaimed, shocked at his appearance. 'Cadet Jacobs, what happened to you?'

Ryan looked down at himself. Standing in the polished hallway, he realised how rough he looked. He was soaked, covered in cuts and bruises and dripping with stagnant mud. The once-white vest was now brown and his trousers had been torn to shreds where the dog had bitten him. The muck fell in clumps on the marble floor. He could only guess what his face looked like, but it wouldn't be pretty.

'I fell in a ditch,' sniffed Ryan. He wiped his eyes with his muddy hand, hoping it wasn't obvious he'd been crying.

'Now, now, cadet,' said Colonel Keller, sneering. 'I think you did much more than that. I think tonight you proved just how untrustworthy you can be.'

The colonel knew something, but Ryan didn't have a clue how much. He couldn't be bothered to argue. 'I guess so,' he admitted, sighing. 'So what happens now?'

'Now?' said the colonel, enjoying the moment. 'Now you find out what happens to people who break the rules.'

24. TRIAL

The head-teacher's office filled with people. Ryan sat in a hard chair in the centre of the room in the filthy remains of his uniform. Lady Devonmoor was upset when she saw the state he was in.

'Colonel Keller,' she had demanded. 'Whatever this is about, I'm sure that Cadet Jacobs doesn't present us with a threat. Uncuff him this instant!'

'Negative,' replied the colonel, unmoving. 'He's guilty of a Class A offence.'

Lady Devonmoor shook her head in disbelief, but didn't argue the point, so Ryan sat there like a criminal as the academy's teachers filtered in. He stared down at his muddy boots, avoiding eye contact.

The room felt warm after the freezing rain outside, and Ryan's clothes started to dry, letting off a rotten stench. It wasn't helping his self-esteem.

He wondered if it had all been worth it, or whether the men were going to kill Lee, now they had what they wanted. He'd done everything he could, but had it been enough?

His worry was short-lived. The door opened and his friend walked in, accompanied by one of the nameless soldiers who patrolled the school grounds.

Ryan cried out in relief. 'Lee! You're alive!'

Lee looked at Ryan. He nodded, embarrassed, but said nothing, constrained as they were by the presence of so many teachers.

It didn't seem possible that Lee should be here already. Ryan had been brought straight here. How had Lee got back so fast? And how had he already got changed into his academy uniform? None of it made sense.

'Well, Colonel, I think we are all here,' said Lady Devonmoor, with a quiet authority. 'We may begin.'

'Of course ma'am,' said the colonel, and he turned to address the room. 'Apologies for summoning you all at such a late hour but we have urgent business to attend to. Cadet Jacobs has committed a Class A offence this evening. As you will be aware, such a breach of the Academy Code requires an immediate decision from all the staff. I am recommending his expulsion from the academy and his return to military custody.'

There were a few murmurs. The colonel pressed on, undeterred. 'You may recall that Cadet Jacobs arrived at this academy following his involvement in a criminal act. He gained unauthorised access to the army's computer network, putting millions of lives in danger. Despite being given the opportunity to reform by being brought here, Jacobs has once again up to his old tricks. He stole dangerous material from the same site, files related to a super-weapon called Project Leopard. He then delivered these files to people he knew to be dangerous.'

'No, no, Colonel, you must be mistaken.' Mr Davids sounded distressed. 'Ryan would do no such thing, would you, Ryan?'

Ryan stayed quiet, afraid to look his mentor in the eye. He felt as dirty as he looked.

Seeing his discomfort, the colonel smirked and carried on: 'Fortunately, this was all a test. There were no dangerous enemies, no terrorists wanting plans to a super-weapon. We set the whole thing up.'

Ryan looked up in shock, as things fell into place. That's how Lee had got back so fast: he had been in the school the whole time! And that's why James Sarrell had been involved. He'd been acting on orders.

Who else had known? Had Lee, Jael or Kev? He didn't think so. Kev would never have cut his feet on the glass if he'd known that it was all a set-up. And Jael wouldn't have been so angry with him for skiving the washing up. As for Lee, Ryan remembered the look on his face when they kidnapped him. He had been scared, really scared.

'What do you mean, Colonel?' Lady Devonmoor asked. 'What did you do?'

'Men from our security detail broke into the boys' dormitory and took Cadet Young captive. Jacobs was then secretly informed that unless he hacked into the army secure network and delivered the Project Leopard files, his friend would be killed.'

'That's outrageous!' Lady Devonmoor stood to her feet, incensed. 'You can't do that! It's emotional blackmail! He's only a boy! What did you expect him to do?'

'I expected him to do exactly what he did,' the colonel replied. 'to put the lives of thousands of other people at risk to save a friend.' Lady Devonmoor opened her mouth as if she was going to speak, then closed it again. The colonel carried on. 'And that is why he can't stay here. He's a liability. If he learns any more about his *trade*,' he almost spat the word, 'then it only gets worse. He needs to be kept in a secure army environment, a place where he can never get near a computer again. Somewhere like Blackfell.'

Ryan shuddered.

'It's entrapment!' The head-teacher moved closer to the colonel, her fiery demeanour staring down his ice-cold expression. 'You can't do that!'

'But I *can* do that.' The colonel sounded triumphant. 'Perhaps Dr Fleur could confirm this for all of us who are present?' He looked up.

'The colonel is right.' Dr Fleur was almost mechanical in her response. 'The academy's constitution allows for the Dean of Discipline to carry out random tests of loyalty and obedience using whatever means he deems necessary to protect the Project. Cadets who fail such tests are subject to usual disciplinary proceedings.'

Lady Devonmoor sank back into her seat, staring murderously at the colonel.

'Cadet Jacobs handed over the plans to a top-secret weapon.' The colonel paced up and down behind Ryan's chair. 'While we might want to say there were exceptional circumstances, we did nothing to him that a potential enemy wouldn't have done. What happens, for instance, if terrorists take his parents hostage? Or if the Outlier kidnaps his friend? This boy, it seems, would betray his entire country to save them. He can't follow the rules, even when breaking them puts thousands of lives at risk.'

'That's not true!' Ryan spat, unable to contain his rage any longer.

'Oh, but it is.' The colonel leaned towards Ryan. 'We know it is because you proved it. You gave confidential plans to dangerous people to save a friend's life. And don't deny it, because I have the proof right here.' The colonel held up the memory stick for everyone to see. 'On this device are the plans to Project Leopard, a military weapon so powerful it could wipe out entire cities. It's all there. I've checked it myself.'

'You've hated Ryan since he came here,' Lady Devonmoor said. 'It's not a fair test.'

'It's more than fair, Lady Devonmoor,' replied the colonel. 'We didn't pretend that he was handing the files to the good guys. He knew they were evil. It didn't stop him. He's a threat to the Project. This incident proves that.'

'The colonel has a point,' agreed Dr Fleur. 'If Jacobs gave confidential military files to terrorists, we would have no option but to expel him and send him back into military custody.'

'He was already on probation,' pointed out Sergeant Wright. 'This would seem to break the terms

171

of that.'

'I-I-I don't know what to say,' spluttered Lady Devonmoor, her outrage subsiding into confusion and disappointment.

The colonel turned to Ryan and narrowed his eyes. 'Well, Jacobs,' he said, with menace. 'It looks like you're finally going to end up where you belong. It's time you went to Blackfell.'

25. CORRUPTED

No-one seemed to know what to say.

Ryan leaned back in the chair. He stretched his muddy legs out in front of him and stared back at the colonel, a defiant look on his face. 'Yeah, well I hate to disappoint you, but I'm not going.'

The colonel gave an evil grin. 'They'll soon knock that arrogance out of you at Blackfell. My only regret is not being there to see it.'

Dr Torren had been watching Ryan with a puzzled expression. 'Something's wrong here,' he said. 'The colonel wants to lock you up and throw away the key, and yet, Cadet Jacobs, you're as cocky as ever. You're not stupid, so I think there's something you haven't told us.'

'Yes, sir,' said Ryan, allowing himself a smile. 'You're right. There is. Colonel Keller is mistaken.'

'How is he mistaken, Ryan?' asked the doctor.

'Because nothing on that device is dangerous. It's all useless data.'

'No! No!' The colonel was on his feet again, angry now. 'More lies! It's all there. I checked it myself!'

'Check it again,' suggested Ryan.

'That seems fair,' said Lady Devonmoor. 'Use my computer, Colonel. Perhaps Mr Davids could look too?'

The colonel strode over to the terminal on Lady Devonmoor's desk and furiously typed away, inserting the memory stick. Mr Davids stood beside him, watching carefully.

'What did you do, Jacobs?' asked Dr Torren, curious.

'I corrupted the file a bit,' explained Ryan. 'But not so anyone would notice on first glance. The diagrams all look ok, the text scans ok, but I randomised most of the numbers. You could never build the weapon using that file, but you wouldn't know until you tried. All the measurements would be useless. The chemistry stuff, that's useless too. And I removed occasional sentences, just in case.'

Dr Torren turned to the two men at the computer. 'Well?'

'The data has been altered as Ryan suggests,' confirmed Mr Davids. 'It looks impressive but the figures are all wrong. Wouldn't you agree, Colonel?'

'So it would seem,' hissed the colonel. He seemed to have difficulty speaking.

'So,' concluded Lady Devonmoor, standing to her feet and taking charge of the situation, 'given that the information he handed to your men was useless, are you charging the boy with anything?'

The colonel stepped away from the desk and answered with as much dignity as he could muster. 'In light of this information, I withdraw the charges against Cadet Jacobs. It seems he has proved himself trustworthy, *this* time at least.' He gave Ryan a look of pure hatred, as if he would tear him to pieces, given half a chance.

'You see, sir,' said Ryan, smiling. 'I can follow the rules. I'm not as bad as you think.' He knew he shouldn't goad the colonel, but it was too good an opportunity to miss.

Colonel Keller's face was getting redder and redder. 'I know *exactly* what you are Jacobs. Enjoy your petty victory. It won't last.' He strode from the room, slamming the door behind him.

'Well, well,' said Lady Devonmoor, 'what a lot of drama for one evening. Lee, dear, could you go to the security desk and fetch the key for those handcuffs?'

'Yes ma'am,' said Lee, grinning at Ryan and dashing off.

As the staff began to disperse, several of them patted Ryan on the shoulder. He wasn't sure whether they were pleased he could stay or just happy to see someone getting one up on the colonel.

Either way, it felt good.

***

'So, what happened to you?' asked Ryan as soon as he and Lee were alone. 'Where have you been?'

'It wasn't too bad,' said Lee. 'I was afraid at first— the shock of it and everything. But they carried me to a room on the other side of the school. They took their masks off and told me that this was all part of a test for you and that I had to stay out of sight for a day or two.'

'I thought they'd thrown you in a dark cell or something!' exclaimed Ryan. 'If I'd known you were safe, I'd never have done any of that!'

'Yeah, well I'm glad that you did,' replied Lee. 'It's nice to know how much you care.' He playfully hit Ryan on the shoulder and Ryan smiled.

As they turned the corner, they were surprised to bump into Dr Torren.

'Ah, Jacobs,' said the doctor, 'that was impressive.'

'Thank you sir,' replied Ryan, glad to have some affirmation at last, but still not sure whose side Dr Torren was on. 'Did you think I'd fail the test?'

The teacher gazed into Ryan's eyes. There was an awkward pause. 'What I think isn't important,' he said. 'What you think is important, Jacobs. And, of course, what you do. Incidentally, Lady Devonmoor has asked me to conduct weekly therapy sessions with you. They will happen every Tuesday at 4pm.'

If this was meant to upset Ryan, he didn't show it. 'Thank you, sir. I look forward to it.'

The teacher looked Ryan up and down, with a slight sense of disapproval. 'Take a shower, Jacobs,' he said, and then carried on down the corridor.

'What was that about?' asked Lee.

'Well, I have PTSD after the car accident and some serious authority issues. They think I can't follow rules. I guess they think therapy will help.'

'I'm not sure about that,' said Lee, in his usual encouraging tone, 'but even if it's true, some things are more important than rules, anyway.'

'Like what?' asked Ryan, surprised to hear Lee say that.

'Like doing the right thing,' Lee shrugged. 'Like friendship.'

'Aw, man, you're going all sentimental on me,' joked Ryan. 'Come on, let's hug...' He moved towards Lee, who recoiled and pushed him away.

'You're kidding, right? You do know you smell like a sewer?'

The two boys stumbled into the dorm room. Ryan was glad to see both Jael and Kev were there.

'Where the hell have you been?' Jael fumed as Ryan walked in, but his anger subsided when he saw Lee.

'Lee!' exclaimed Kev. 'You're safe!'

Lee grinned at his friends. 'Did you miss me?'

They explained everything that had happened, from the time Lee had been abducted right up to the trial in Lady Devonmoor's office.

'So you see, Jael,' said Ryan, summing up. 'I didn't have any choice but to leave you in the kitchen.'

'That's a good excuse, man,' Jael admitted, a slight smile at the corner of his mouth. 'But that washing up took me hours! I mean, next time we're on duty you can do it on your own, and I get to pour gravy over you!'

Ryan laughed. 'Deal!' he agreed, and they shook on it. He'd have done the clean-up shift ten times over if it meant that Jael would forgive him.

'I think you need to get cleaned up before lights out!' suggested Kev. 'You're stinking the whole place out! And look at the state of your uniform!'

'What, seriously?' Ryan gave him a mischievous look. 'You think I'm dirty? I don't think it's too bad. I was going to wear this to drill.'

Jael shot a meaningful glance at Kev before launching himself at Ryan, beating him with his pillow.

'Ok, ok,' spluttered Ryan, as he fought off Jael's attack. 'I'll change! I promise!'

'And have a shower?' demanded Jael, standing over him with the pillow raised.

'Sure. If you insist!'

As Ryan stripped off the filthy clothes, he looked at his new friends, laughing and chatting with one another now that the ordeal was over.

You're right, Lee, thought Ryan. *Some things are more important than the rules.*

EPILOGUE

It was a few days later when Ryan next encountered Sarrell.

The canteen was packed with people. Ryan sat at a table with his food. He'd scored three out of five on the canteen test which had earned him a plate of lasagne.

Sparks was in mid-flow, telling an entertaining story about an invention which had gone wrong and set fire to the engineering block. Lee was sitting next to Ryan, laughing as he heard how Sparks had accidentally soaked the teacher with the fire extinguisher. Everyone seemed relaxed and life was good.

But suddenly Sparks paused, a worried look on his face. Something was wrong.

And then Ryan felt it.

Cold liquid ran through his hair and down his back, soaking his uniform. As it made its way into his trousers, Ryan turned to face James Sarrell, who was standing behind him, grinning.

'So sorry, Jacobs, it slipped out of my hands. Again.'

Ryan glanced around. Everyone was watching.

'No problem, James,' Ryan said, picking up his

own drink. 'Here, have mine. Or you could pour it on me as well if you like? I don't mind.'

He leaned back against the table, making himself an easy target, half-expecting Sarrell to do just that. Weirdly, he didn't care.

But the bully was caught off guard. He didn't understand what was going on. Bewildered, he took the drink from Ryan and retreated from the table.

The small crowd that had gathered began to disperse. Ryan noticed Sarah Devonmoor linger a while longer than the others. She stared at him for a few moments before turning away. He wasn't sure if he'd imagined it but she may have smiled.

As Ryan turned back to his meal, he saw the look on Lee's face. 'What?' he asked.

'You're confusing, that's all,' replied Lee.

'Do you think he'll do it again?' asked Ryan.

'Probably. Sarrell's a bully. Chances are he hasn't finished with you. The question is, what will you do next time?'

'Ah, well,' said Ryan. 'I'd tell you, but I wouldn't want to ruin the surprise.'

If Ryan was being honest, he didn't know. He doubted that he'd always be able to control his anger like that. At some point he'd snap.

But, he had to admit, it felt good not getting into trouble.

And it felt good having nothing to prove.

GET YOUR FREE E-BOOK

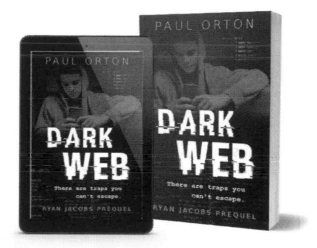

There are traps you can't escape.

When Ryan Jacobs asks to join the Faction he finds himself trapped in a situation which keeps getting worse. He needs to escape fast, or they will own him forever. But how can he fight an invisible enemy?

Find out about Ryan's life before he is taken to the Academy. DARK WEB is exclusively available to members of the Ryan Jacobs Alliance – sign up for free at www.paulorton.net

A NOTE FROM THE AUTHOR

Thanks for reading 'The Rules'. If you're up for more of Ryan's adventures, very soon I will be releasing the next book in the series: *Wild Fury*. In it, Ryan is tested to the limit.

Can't wait until then? The great news is: you don't have to! There's another Ryan Jacobs book you can read *right now!* It's called *Dark Web* and it's exclusive to members of my readers' club – the Ryan Jacobs Alliance. You can join for free and not only will you get to find out what Ryan's life was like before he arrived at Devonmoor Academy, but I'll also keep you up to date with new releases! Visit www.paulorton.net to join.

And could you do me a huge favour? I need you to review *The Rules* right now on Amazon. Reviews make a huge difference to a new author like me, and it would be amazing if you could write a sentence or two about what you liked about it. I'd really appreciate it and I promise I read every review.

Until next time,

Paul.

RYAN JACOBS BOOK 2

They call it the Fury. And no-one is safe.

Life has got very complicated for Ryan. The fact is that he's never been much of a team player. It's not easy when your friends hate you and everyone else is on your case. And that was before people started going crazy. He has to find some answers, and fast. Before things get out of hand. Before anyone gets killed. Or worse.

WILD FURY is the second book in the Ryan Jacobs series and will be released soon. To stay up to date, join the Ryan Jacobs Alliance, and you'll also get a free e-book. Find out more at <u>www.paulorton.net</u>

Printed in Great Britain
by Amazon

66634727R00111